Extraordinary praise for *Redemption in Indigo:*

★ "A great deal happens in the novel's relatively short course, but confusion is minimal because Lord has found the ideal voice for the narrator—feminine yet authoritative, amusing yet soothing, omniscient yet humble. This is one of those literary works of which it can be said that not a word should be changed."
—*Booklist* (Starred Review)

★ "Packs a great deal of subtly alluring storytelling into this small package…. An unnamed narrator, sometimes serious and often mischievous, spins delicate but powerful descriptions of locations, emotions, and the protagonists' great flaws and great strengths as they interact with family, poets, tricksters, sufferers of tragedy, and—of course—occasional moments of pure chaos."—*Publishers Weekly* (Starred Review)

Top 10 Best Science Fiction and Fantasy of the Year—Amazon.com

"There's never a doubt we're in the hands of a contemporary taleteller with a voice both insouciant and respectful of its sources, and it's a voice we'd like to hear more from. *Redemption in Indigo* is wise, funny, and very promising."—*Locus*

"Very sprightly from start to finish, with vivid descriptions, memorable heroes and villains, brisk pacing—and an "authorised" epilogue that raises goosebumps along with expectations for a sequel. . . . That's clever storytelling."—*Caribbean Review of Books*

"Full of sharp insights and humorous asides ("I know your complaint already. You are saying, how do two grown men begin to see talking spiders after only three glasses of spice spirit?"), *Redemption* extends the Caribbean Island storyteller's art into the 21st century and hopefully, beyond."—*Seattle Times*

"Unique, warm, funny, and smart, and her speculative imaginings should awaken every fantasy fan's sense of wonder. It might not make it to a bestseller list, but given time, it might be found on a list of hidden gems—as might whatever Lord writes next."—*Reflection's Edge*

"Drawing on a multicultural mélange of narrative traditions—both oral and written—this Barbadian author surprises. She tap dances across the conventional, using it to make spirited sounds. She twists out of tired modes: "Once upon a time—but whether a time that was, or a time that is, or a time that is to come, I may not tell." Then, Lord ends the tale by challenging "those who utterly, utterly fear the dreaded Moral of the Story." Expect a work that can revive this and other exhausted elements of story."—*Foreword Reviews*

Redemption in Indigo

Redemption in Indigo

a novel

Karen Lord

Small Beer Press
Easthampton, MA

To the memory of my mother, Muriel Haynes Lord.

Redemption in Indigo copyright © 2010 by Karen Lord. All rights reserved.
merumsal.wordpress.com

Chapters two, three and four of this novel are loosely based on a Senegalese folk tale set down by Leo Frobenius (1873-1938) in *Atlantis: Volksmärchen und Volksdichtungen Afrikas*, Vol. 6, (Jena: E. Diederichs, 1921-28).

Small Beer Press
150 Pleasant Street #306
Easthampton, MA 01027
www.smallbeerpress.com
www.weightlessbooks.com
info@smallbeerpress.com

Distributed to the trade by Consortium.

Library of Congress Cataloging-in-Publication Data

Library of Congress Cataloging-in-Publication Data

Lord, Karen, 1968-
  Redemption in indigo : a novel / Karen Lord. -- 1st ed.
    p. cm.
  ISBN 978-1-931520-66-9 (alk. paper)
  I. Title.
  PR9230.9.L67R43 2010
  813'.6--DC22

                          2009054298

First edition   2 3 4 5 6 7 8 9

Printed on 50# 30% recycled paper by Thomson-Shore of Dexter, MI.
Text set in Centaur 12 PT.
Author photo © 2010 by Risée N. C. Chaderton (www.eyerisee.com).
Cover photo © 2010 by Corbis.

Introduction

A RIVAL OF MINE ONCE complained that my stories begin awkwardly and end untidily. I am willing to admit to many faults, but I will not burden my conscience with that one. All my tales are true, drawn from life, and a life story is not a tidy thing. It is a half-tamed horse that you seize on the run and ride with knees and teeth clenched, and then you regretfully slip off as gently and safely as you can, always wondering if you could have gone a few metres more.

Thus I seize this tale, starting with a hot afternoon in the town of Erria, a dusty side street near the financial quarter. But I will make one concession to tradition...

...Once upon a time—but whether a time that was, or a time that is, or a time that is to come, I may not tell—there was a man, a tracker by occupation, called Kwame. He had been born in a certain country in a certain year when history had reached that grey twilight in which fables of true love, the power of princes, and deeds of honour are told only to children. He regretted this oversight on the part of Fate, but he managed to curb his restless imagination and do the daily work that brought in the daily bread.

Today's work will test his self-restraint.

'How long has she been...absent?' he asked his clients.

In spite of his tact, they looked uncomfortable, but that was

1

to be expected of a housekeeper and butler tasked by their master to trace his missing wife, a woman named Paama. 'Nearly two years,' replied the housekeeper. 'She said she was going to visit her family, but the entire family has moved away from Erria,' the butler explained. 'No forwarding address,' the housekeeper whispered, as if ashamed. 'Mister Ansige is distraught.'

Kwame eyed the pair, then glanced down at the papers before him. These were letters from minor chiefs and high-ranking officials politely demanding his assistance. If nothing else, Mister Ansige was well connected. It was a tawdry shadow of the power he had dreamed of—was the true love of this deserted husband similarly tarnished? And what of his own honour? He was very wary of trying to find people who did not wish to be found, but the names on those scraps of paper ensured that any refusal from him would not be quickly forgotten.

Fairy tales and nancy stories, his adult self said, trying to sneer at these scruples before he had time to question whether it was cowardice or prudence that made him cautious. *Do the work and stop your dreaming.*

'I'll see what I can do,' he sighed with a faint grimace.

He had little choice. The rent of an office, even in a town like Erria, was more than his business could support, and he needed this case to conclude his affairs honestly before he could resume his itinerant ways. He yearned for those days of walking free, with not a townman to pressure him about which case to take and which trail to leave. Leaner days, too, if truth be told, but Kwame had always found liberty more satisfying than comfort.

Poor Paama, his conscience murmured. *Do you want to go back, or do you prefer liberty, too?*

＊

While Kwame is sniffing out the trail of Ansige's wife, let us run ahead of him and meet her for ourselves. She and her family have resettled in Makendha, the village of her childhood. Much is familiar there, little has changed except, of course, for those who return.

Paama's father, Semwe, had left when a youth, returned, then left again when a man. Now an elder, he will never leave again ... at least not the mortal part of him. He had wanted this final return to be a peaceful retirement; he acknowledged with regret that it was a retreat. The townhouse in Erria had lost all peace with regular visits from messengers bearing Ansige's variously phrased demands for Paama's return. Semwe refused to argue with such a man, preferring to go to a place of quiet and safety where unwanted company could be more easily avoided. In a town, houses crowd together and everyone is a stranger, but in Makendha, a stranger was anyone who could not claim relation to four generations' worth of bones in the local churchyard.

Semwe's wife, Tasi, was coming to Makendha for the second time, no longer the timid young wife, but not yet the matriarch. She needed grandchildren for that, and how, she murmured, blaming herself, could she get those while her daughters stayed husbandless? She had no hope that Paama's marriage could be salvaged. She had chosen poorly for her first child, and she only prayed that she might choose more wisely for the other. Paama at least had strength and experience to sustain her, but her sister, Neila, ten years younger, had only a combination of beauty and self-centredness that both attracted and repelled. She took the move from Erria as a personal attack on her God-given right to a rich, handsome husband. Tasi deplored such selfishness but silently admitted that prospects in Makendha were certainly limited.

And what of Paama herself? She said little about the husband she had left almost two years ago, barely enough to fend off the village gossips and deflect her sister's sneers. She didn't need to. There was something else about Paama that distracted people's attention from any potentially juicy titbits of her past. She could cook.

An inadequate statement. Anyone can cook, but the true talent belongs to those who are capable of gently ensnaring with their delicacies, winning compliance with the mere suggestion that there might not be any goodies for a caller who persisted in prying. Such was Paama. She had always had a knack, but the promise had come to full flower through constant practice. It was also a way for her to thank her family. Life, even life without grandchildren and a pair of rich, handsome sons-in-law, could be sweet when there was a savoury stew gently bubbling on the stove, rice with a hint of jasmine steaming in the pot, and honey cakes browning in the oven. It almost cured Semwe's stoically silent worry, Tasi's guilty fretting, and Neila's bitter sighs.

Besides, it kept Paama busy enough to ignore the nagging question of how she was going to tell Ansige she was never coming back. She will have to consider that question soon, for efficient Kwame has already traced her whereabouts and, not without a qualm, reported to Ansige.

And Ansige, in his desperation, will not be sending messages or servants this time. He is coming to speak to her, face to face.

'Is that the one?'

'It is. She is.'

'I don't see it.'

There was a meaningful silence. It said a lot about what might not be seen by such minor beings as the first speaker. The quiet rebuke was absorbed with equal quietness, and then the first speaker tried again.

'Ansige is on the way. He is coming to fetch her back.'

'Delay him. She will be strong enough to deal with him by the time he arrives, and she will only grow stronger from there on. Then, when they meet, watch, and you will see. She alone can safely wield the power that I shall take from our ... former colleague.' The last two words rode on the breath of a regretful sigh.

'Will you really? I mean, to involve a human! Are you certain?'

'I am certain that Paama can wield it, and I am equally certain that *he* must not. Isn't that enough?'

Another pause, then, 'He is going to be very angry. He will try his utmost to get it back.'

The reply held a subtle glimmer of a smile. 'That is indeed my hope.'

These two unknown figures have plans for Paama, fate like plans in which Ansige, if he is not careful, will be brushed aside like a fly. It is the pause point of the wave at its crest, the rumbling of a distant storm, the thrill in the backbone when the eyes of the predator glitter in the moonlight from the darkness of the trees and tall grass. Something is going to change, and it is for you to judge at the end of the tale who has made the best of the change and of their choices.

1

ANSIGE IS DELAYED ON THE ROAD TO MAKENDHA

WHY DID PAAMA LEAVE ANSIGE?

There are men of violence. There are men who drink. And then there was Ansige, a man with a vice so pathetic as to be laughable. He ate; he lived for his belly. No one would believe that a woman could leave a man for that, but before you scoff, consider this. With his gluttony, he drew in other sins—arrogance complicated by indolent stupidity, lust for comfort, ire when thwarted, avarice in all his business dealings, and a strange conviction that always, somehow, there was some undeserving person who had more food than he did.

I can hear some of you complaining already. 'A woman who cooks and a man who eats should be a match made in heaven!' Do you really think so? Then you have not grasped that Ansige was not an epicure, but a gourmand. Paama's talents were wasted on him.

Whatever his faults, he was not yet so far gone in discourtesy as to try turning up unannounced. Unfortunately, the messenger who brought the tidings to Makendha made sure that everyone knew, and wherever Paama went, she heard this half query:

'I hear that your husband is coming to Makendha.'

Paama's usual response to this was to breathe deeply, gather herself, and beam forth a brilliant smile. 'Isn't it marvellous? When I visit my family he gets so lonely. He cannot do without me.'

7

Any gossip thus treated would then tilt her head doubtfully, smile uncertainly, and go away dissatisfied. The village longed for word on just what was the situation with Paama's marriage, but no-one could break past Paama when she decided to be earnest. She had the talent of speaking many things with little meaning, the gift of red herrings.

Fortunately she did not have to red-herring the gossips about the date of his arrival. Ansige was one week late, turning up all but unexpected, looking around for his welcoming committee. But no, before we describe his arrival, it would be worthwhile to relate the event that caused the delay, for it was rather unusual and makes a good story in itself.

Ansige had set out with an entourage as grand as any minor chief. He had a veritable herd of quadrupeds—eight mules for his baggage and one horse for him to ride. Amid the baggage were bundled sections of wood which, when assembled, would become the light carriage in which he would make his grand entrance into Makendha.

He couldn't help himself. His mother had been the daughter of a minor chief, and she had carefully instilled in Ansige an understanding of the importance of importance. Dutiful son, he followed this instruction to the letter, for the longer the baggage train, the more of his favourite foods he could carry with him.

This is not to say that Ansige was above living off the land, which was why his two mule drivers were both expert hunters, and one was also a reasonably talented chef. The household of Ansige had many such multiskilled persons—a side effect of Ansige's curious mingling of parsimony and ostentatiousness.

Experienced in providing for Ansige, they had brought a formidable array of equipment. They carried with them both the long throwing spears needed for swift, running game and the short thrusting spears most effective with ground-crawling game. One was skilled with the bow, the other with a blowpipe, and the points of their arrows and darts had been dipped in poison. There was material for fashioning traps and snares; hooks and a quantity of fishing line for when they travelled alongside the river; assorted scaling, skinning, jointing, dressing, and carving knives; and racks and bags for the hunters to carry their kill to camp.

It is not necessary to discuss the pots, pans, cutlery and crockery. These are not worth commenting on; they were very basic since Ansige was not particularly interested in the presentation once the food was tasty and plentiful. Besides, a little privation was to be expected during travel.

This, as you can appreciate, implied a leisurely trip, for who has time to move quickly while hunting and then cooking so much meat? However, Ansige did not expect the hunters to be out every day. They were his insurance, a safety net in case anything should happen to the food stores.

In fact, the bulk of the baggage was food. Five bags of coarsely ground meal, two bags of finely ground meal, and one bag of sugar covered the backs of one mule pair, while ten packets of dried fruit, twenty dozen eggs (carefully packed in a hay-stuffed crate), and seven sacks of rice weighed down another. Further down, there were three crates of dried, salted fish and two boxes of dried, salted beef. These provided the base for the large pot of highly seasoned pepperpot, which was placed on the campfire at every lunch and dinner, but fresh meat was also used to replenish the stock. Smaller boxes contained assorted sweetmeats and delicacies for Ansige to munch on; packets of spice tree bark to brew Ansige's favourite drink; and—the *pièce de résistance*—a bottle of strong sugar brandy, for medicinal purposes.

Now you understand why Ansige had sent messages and servants to Paama. Travel was for him a serious and frightening undertaking which threatened to pinch off the umbilical cord that kept him tethered to his house. His journey to Makendha would take only three days, but he had taken every precaution so as not to arrive haggard and starved out.

Truth to tell, his frame looked as if it would take far more than three days' worth of racking to pare it down. Ansige was not flabby, no, but he was solid. Layers of muscle braced the fat around his arms, legs, and shoulders. Only his belly betrayed him. He carried a prosperous paunch before him and occasionally stroked it as fondly as any expectant mother cradling her womb.

A prosperous, slightly pompous businessman, then, was the first impression Ansige gave to strangers. Ansige's outer appearance could be deceptive, but, given enough time, he let everyone know who and what he was.

There are people who inspire others to reach lofty goals. Ansige was one of these. People got to know him, and it came to them in a flash of revelation that whatever it was that they wanted to be, it was not a man like Ansige, and they scrambled to occupy the opposite end of the accomplishment spectrum. People have heroes whom they imitate; Ansige was the perfect anti hero. No-one wanted to turn out like him.

How then, you may ask, and wisely so, were Paama and her parents so thoroughly fooled? They do not appear to be stupid people. There again we must thank Ansige's mother. She had come to realise that the only way Ansige was going to give her any grandchildren was if she sent him to a place reasonably distant where no-one had heard of him or seen his follies. She had selected Paama in Erria for her famous cooking, and then she had rented a small restaurant nearby so that she could stuff Ansige's roaring appetite silent before sending him off, sated and sane, to woo Paama and impress her family. I do not doubt that she may have had her more royal relatives speak to the chief of Makendha and the bureaucrats of Erria and encourage them to pass on to Paama's family a good report of her son. What else could she have done? It is a heavy burden, as Paama's parents had found out, to find a worthy spouse for one's offspring, but how much harder the task and heavier the burden when not even love can hide from a doting mother's eyes the sad fact of her son's utter ineligibility.

Now that you have seen Ansige and heard something of his background, imagine the temper of a man like that when he finds a wash of landslid mud has covered the road ahead of him, the road leading to Makendha. First the pangs of fear and frustration hit his belly, so in an instant he is fishing in his saddlebags for something to chew on and settle his nervous stomach. Then he feels strong enough to start flinging blame about. He blames his mule-driving hunters for having selected the road. He blames them further for not having known in advance of its condition. He blames the Council of Chiefs for permitting roads to get into such a condition, and then he blames the Parliament of Princes for allowing such ineffectual chiefs to stay in power. He blames Paama's family for moving to such a distant village, and Paama for staying such a long time with them, and his servants for being so bad at running his household that he has been forced to go fetch his wife. Finally he blames God for the weather, and that, as you know, is the point at which mere pettiness descends into dangerous folly.

Rahid, the mule-driving hunter who was not a chef, grinned. Do not be fooled by his happy face. Rahid is a pure cynic who has long ago concluded that since the world seems set up for men like Ansige to get ahead, the only thing to do is to work for the most amusing one of the breed so that one can at least be entertained by his japes and capers. Of course he is not correct, but it will take a broader experience than his home village and its environs for him to learn otherwise.

'What do you recommend, Mister Ansige?' he enquired.

'I? Recommend?' Ansige spat fragments of food in his wrath. 'It is for you to tell me how you plan to get me out of this mess that you have got me into!'

Pei, the mule-driving hunter who *was* a chef, looked disgusted, an unwise beginning since it only made Ansige think that he must be against him.

Pei said, 'It is a half day's trip to Erria in the north. Let us go there and see if anyone knows of a better road, or if they will help us to clear this one.'

Dissatisfied by this suggestion, Ansige turned to Rahid instead and allowed himself to be soothed by that crocodile smile. Rahid was shaking his head. He knew already what Ansige was thinking.

'Erria is a small town, and we may be waiting there for some time before we can continue our journey. It does not have the kind of lodgings that you would appreciate, and we will soon run through—I mean run out of the food we have brought. Let us go instead to Ahani in the east. The journey will take a day and a half, but it is a large city and there will be good roads directly to Makendha. We can even get provisions while we are there.'

Ansige brightened up. Any disappointment could be overcome by the prospect of a good feed, and after two days on the road, he had been eyeing the stores uneasily. He was almost out of chocolate-covered fire ants, and he would miss their snap and crunch for his evening's appetiser.

Naturally they headed for Ahani.

For a moment I need to mention our as-yet-anonymous pair who wanted to see Ansige delayed. You do not know who they are, but I would not have you think badly of them out of ignorance, so just bear in mind that the only thing they arranged was the delay. The choice to go to Erria or to Ahani lay in the hands of the travellers, and only the travellers are responsible for what happened next.

When they reached Ahani, Ansige was weary, but not as weary

as Rahid and Pei. Ansige's freshly awakened anxiety meant that they had endured a lifetime of childish, whining complaints until Pei had had the bright idea of leaving in a tiny trace of the poison sac of the bleerfrog when he prepared its legs for Ansige's breakfast. The result had been a slow, unusually silent Ansige, too tired to be fretful, who struggled to stay awake in the saddle. They quickly found lodgings and rolled him into bed, placing a few covered dishes in the room in case he should revive and remember his stomach before dinner. Then they left him and went to the nearest bar to drink to their shared misery.

First Rahid bought a drink for them both, and they grew more cheerful. Then Pei bought a drink for them both, and on that they grew indignant, telling tale after tale of the madness that was a man's life in the service of Ansige. Then a third round arrived, and they did not know who was paying for it, but when they looked around, there was a friendly-looking spider of more than average size who raised his glass cheerfully in their direction and indicated with a wave that they should go ahead and drink up on his behalf. Heartened by such a gesture of diplomacy from a representative of the animal kingdom, they toasted him gladly and resumed their tales of woe to each other.

'I tell you, I do not think I can stand this for one day more,' confided Rahid.

'You?' Pei exclaimed. 'You are always smiling! You are his favourite, you and your peaceful, happy smile!'

'I smile so that I do not weep or try to grind his head between my jaws. But now my face is tired and I am thinking to myself, is this really all there is to life, to wait on the Ansiges of the world until they drop dead from the excesses of their addictions? We are in Ahani, friend, a city of many entertainments, and all we can do is snatch a moment in a downtown bar because our boss is lying half-drugged in his bed. Why are we doomed to follow this man like nursemaids of an overgrown baby?'

Pei sipped at his glass and thought. Rahid had never called him 'friend' before, but it was a word that went well with the flavour of the spiced alcohol. 'You surprise me. And yet, even before you spoke, I thought to myself, "We are indeed in Ahani, and there are many roads that lead from here." Many, many roads.'

He smiled at his glass. It seemed to be in on the joke. It fed daring and plausibility to the tiny flame of rebellion growing in his heart.

Rahid was also staring at his drink as if there were inspiration in its dregs. 'I am not a thief. We can put the mules in pawn, draw out our last wages, and leave the rest of the money with Ansige.'

'We are fair men,' Pei agreed. 'We can make all the arrangements before we go—for his lodging, his provisioning, and his onward transport. Thus we discharge our duties for this trip.'

'Gentlemen, pardon me for eavesdropping.'

It was the spider. He was a handsome specimen, standing well over a metre at the shoulder, and he had a slight tendency to gesticulate upward with his front legs that made him appear taller. His eyes were keen and deep, and they radiated sympathy.

'I could not help overhearing you, and I thought to myself that I might be of some assistance, for I am a pawnbroker.'

Rahid and Pei looked at each other and nodded. This made perfect sense.

'I will pawn just the second mule pair of the train. It is practically mine anyway,' said Pei.

'And I will pawn the hunting gear, which I have made mine through years of use,' said Rahid.

Thus, with feelings of honesty and honour intact, they made their transactions and agreed to meet the spider in a few minutes for the exchange of goods and cash. They returned to the hotel, where Ansige dreamed on in ignorance, and they settled his bill for three days in advance. After thoughtfully leaving a note of explanation for Ansige, they proceeded to the pawnbroker's office to get their wages cashed.

I know your complaint already. You are saying, how do two grown men begin to see talking spiders after only three glasses of spice spirit? My answer to that is twofold. First, you have no idea how strong spice spirit is made in that region. Second, you have no idea how talking animals operate. Do you think they would have survived long if they regularly made themselves known? For that matter, do you think an arachnid with mouthparts is capable of articulating the phrase 'I am a pawnbroker' in any known human language? Think! These creatures do not truly talk, nor are they truly animals, but they do encounter human folk, and when they do, they carefully take with them all memory of the meeting.

To resume, by evening Pei and Rahid had departed the city, still riding the buzz of the alcohol's inspiration. Pei went north to the desert, and Rahid south to the sea, and I have no further report of them for the time being. I do know that they never spoke of the spider again, though they did have vague memories of a hairy pawnbroker, very well endowed in the arm department, with keen, deep, sympathetic eyes.

In the meantime, Ansige awoke and found his servants gone. He went to the hotel proprietor and was told there was a note, but then the note could not be found and seemed to have blown away. Ansige, who was not a hard-hearted man, took it into his head that his two servants had stepped out briefly and been waylaid and probably murdered by vicious city thugs. He became so upset at this picture that instead of doing the sensible thing, which would have been to inform the authorities, he shut himself up for two days of constant room service and ran up such a bill that even the generous prepayment arranged by Pei and Rahid could not cover it.

Now you understand how we come at last to this quite different picture of a delayed, distressed Ansige departing for Makendha. He was forced to sell the mules and the majority of the baggage, partly to pay his bill and partly because he could not afford to hire anyone to take care of them on the onward journey. He did not wish to part with the horse, but the hotel proprietor convinced him that he should leave it behind to be rented out so it could pay for its own keep until Ansige returned. Pei and Rahid's plans for transport had to be scrapped. Now that he lacked a chef, he needed to get to Makendha as quickly as possible so as not to miss any proper meals.

Driven by the mania of his obsession and blinded by the melancholy of loneliness, Ansige made his choices and boarded a five-hour omnibus to Makendha with nothing more than a small suitcase and a packet of antinausea, antacid chews. Then, because he still had quite a large amount of money, he hopped off briefly at the first stop to buy food, just in case his stomach recovered during the trip.

2

ANSIGE EATS LAMB AND MURDERS A PEACOCK

SEMWE HEADED ANSIGE OFF BEFORE he could come to their door and ushered him into the village's guest lodge. For the sake of his daughter, he tried to talk as if he were really glad to see Ansige. 'How nice to see you again. Did you have a pleasant journey?'

It was the perfect trigger. Ansige unreeled the tale of his tribulations, thoroughly ransacking the truth and then dipping into the bag of embellishment and sprinkling with a free hand. He noted how Semwe's face grew agonised in sympathy at hearing that such a horrible experience could happen to anyone in a supposedly safe country. He was only partially correct. Semwe was counting under his breath with a kind of furious amazement at the fact that Ansige had been talking nonstop for twenty-five minutes with no more encouragement than a glazed look.

'You must be hungry,' he interjected desperately.

It was the perfect distraction. Ansige choked off in midflow and murmured weakly that yes, he was indeed rather famished.

'I have the perfect solution. Come with me.'

Semwe led him from the lodge to the edge of his own field, where a young lamb was tethered.

'Yours,' he told Ansige, untying the cord and hooking the loops over Ansige's eagerly outstretched hand. 'It will make a good dinner.

Take it, tie it in the court in front of the lodge for now. I must go tell
Paama you are here.'

Off he went to find Paama and tell her about Ansige's arrival. It
took him a while because Paama had already seen Ansige from a distance and didn't want to be found. Eventually she relented, to spare
her family the shame of a grown daughter hiding like a child.

'Besides,' she said to herself, 'if I know my husband, it will not
take him long to get into very deep trouble.'

She went to the lodge, but to her surprise he was not there. She
began to wander through the village, looking for him with more duty
than enthusiasm. Finally she made herself widen the search to the
fields. By then twilight was deepening to dusk, so rather than go far,
Paama decided she would only visit her family's lands. The moment
she saw what was happening there, she clapped her hands over her
mouth for one frozen moment of horror and then started to run.

So that you may understand what has happened, we must go
back to the moment when Semwe left Ansige holding the lamb by its
tether. You will recall that Ansige was supposed to take it back to the
court outside the lodge. Well, he did take one step, but then his stomach snarled at him, and his thoughts ran thus:

He was really hungry.

If he took the lamb back to the lodge, he would be compelled by
courtesy to share it with any other guests staying there.

He was practically starving, and he did not want to do this.

Semwe gave the lamb to *him*. Why shouldn't he enjoy it by
himself?

He looked around, and there was a corner of ruined old wall,
and in its shadow a space of blackened earth and stone. Someone had
lit a fire there once, and so could he. Tugging the protesting beast after
him, he went back and forth across the field, gathering sticks and grass
and other fuel, and heaping them up by the sheltering bricks of the

old, broken wall. Then he drew out his knife and rolled up his sleeves.

Anyone who has ever butchered an animal will not need to have the messy business described. They will, however, wonder whatever possessed Ansige to opt for hastily butchered, half-barbecued, unseasoned carcass of lamb when he could have had a proper meal shared with his fellow human beings. I will not try to explain his behaviour. I have already made it quite clear that the man has problems, and so we cannot expect him to act logically.

It was not even this scene that caused Paama's reaction. It so happened that after Ansige somehow managed to pick the lamb down to well-gnawed bones, he still felt cravings. He looked around for something to ... well ... not pack the empty spaces, for they were already packed, but to give his stomach that pleasantly stretched sensation without which he always felt slightly uneasy. His eyes anxiously scanned the flat lands from horizon to horizon until he saw a sheep, half-hidden amid a clump of tall khus-khus grass.

No, he won't, I hear you saying. Make him a glutton, make him a fool, but do not make him a thief, for we cannot believe that such a man would stoop to larceny. Very well, let me once again explain his thoughts, but I do not want to have to do this too often. He employs a twisted kind of logic, but one that still works when the will is looking for any excuse. Thus runs the train of his reasoning:

Thought 1: I am Semwe's guest.

Thought 2: It is Semwe's responsibility to feed his guest.

Thought 3: These are Semwe's lands.

Thought 4: The sheep is on Semwe's lands and is therefore Semwe's sheep, and so I can eat it.

Don't be startled at the galloping logic in the last thought. The will is usually in a hurry to get to the point of justification.

His blunted conscience nudged him slightly. Was that sheep really Semwe's? His whole argument swung on that point, and if the reasoning-out of his actions was not firmly grounded, the uncertainty might interfere with his digestion. He looked around for some way out of this difficulty and caught sight of a stick insect, commonly known as a godhorse.

The godhorse had perched itself on the top of the cracked remnants of the wall, downwind of the smoke from the dying fire. It wagged its head slowly from side to side and looked at Ansige very sternly. It was not this that made Ansige stare at it, however. It was the manner in which it sat: back curled like a young twig, lower legs lapped, midlegs bracing it as it leaned back, and front legs folded.

Ansige goggled a moment longer and then found his voice. 'Pardon me, but—'

'Yes, these are Semwe's lands,' said the godhorse in a solemn, almost bored voice.

'Oh. Then perhaps you know if—'

'And the sheep, as any fool can see, is standing on Semwe's lands,' said the creature coldly.

'Oh. So then it is certainly Semwe's sheep.'

There was a tense silence while the godhorse glared at him. Finally it said, 'That wasn't a question.'

'I . . . what? But—'

'I don't wish to talk to you any more, you . . . you . . . ,' snapped the godhorse, but it was a tired attempt at scolding that trailed off as if it considered Ansige unworthy of the breath and effort of a proper insult.

It uncricked its joints and stalked away into the grass, where it soon disappeared among the sticks and straw of brown and gold. Ansige immediately forgot it had spoken. All he remembered was that someone had told him this was Semwe's sheep, so anything that he planned for it was bound to be in order. Conscience appeased, he jumped up from the scant leavings of his meal and went to grab the next course, but to his surprise it moved off, trailing a frayed line of cord behind it. He headed it off and made another grab, but it stepped out of the way. A slow-motion chase ensued, a parody of a hunt—full, lumbering Ansige after the sedate sheep, whose mission in life seemed to be to discover the most economical movements that would put it mere millimetres beyond Ansige's reach.

Panting, pouring sweat, he halted for a moment to catch his breath. He slowly turned around, surveying the fields, and stopped short at a horrific sight. There was a bird, a huge, sleek, colourful, bold-faced bird, picking away at the scraps of meat he had left behind! He was still staring at it, too appalled to move, when a thin, dry chuckle caught his ear. It was the arthritic godhorse, now seated on a low boundary stone nearby.

'I wouldn't take that if I were you,' it mocked him, jerking a limb at the scavenging bird. 'A fat bird like that should make a good meal, don't you think?'

With that comment, Ansige reached the pinnacle of frustration. He picked up a rock, hurled it, and whacked the thieving bird on its tiny brainpan. It fell dead instantly.

Now enter Paama. Poor thing. She came running towards Ansige, trying to scream out her dismay in a kind of anguished whisper.

'Are you mad? Where is the lamb my father gave you? Why have you killed the village peacock?'

Ansige looked at her, looked at the peacock, and looked at her again. The day's injustices seemed to pile up in his throat as he tried to explain to her that it was a perfectly natural mistake that anyone could have made, and why did she have to scold him for it? His emotions spilled out in an indignant bluster.

'Don't act as if you don't know me! I ate the lamb your father gave me, but it wasn't enough, so I saw the sheep and I thought he wouldn't mind if I had a little extra sustenance. He knows what a hard time I had coming here. And then this bird started eating the best bits of *my* leftovers that I hadn't really finished with, and anyway, if it was the village peacock, why wasn't it kept in a cage instead of being allowed to wander about stealing people's food?'

And Ansige put on one of his famous expressions, the one titled 'I have been Unwarrantedly Injured and Unreasonably Slandered.'

Paama was far too accustomed to the look for it to have any effect, and too horrified at the sight of the dead peacock. 'Ansige, the chief will have you punished for killing our peacock! This is a rare bird, a gift from a visiting prince. He has walked about the village unmolested for years, and you manage to dispose of him within one day of being here! I have to find a way to get you out of this.'

'Well, if you had fed me properly—' he began petulantly.

'Be quiet,' said Paama, looking around frantically. 'See there? That horse tethered over there has not yet been broken in. You must take the peacock and lay him near the horse's hooves. Then I will scream loudly, people will come running, and we will tell them the horse kicked the peacock and killed him.'

Ansige grumbled and whined and was fearful of coming near the hooves of the wild horse, but Paama bullied and persuaded him. He crept closer with the bloodied body in his hands, but the horse moved skittishly aside and tossed its head up, scaring him into retreat. Then, just as Ansige made a rush forward and dropped the bird on the ground, the horse decided it had had enough. Neighing an indignant scream, it reared up at Ansige, who screamed in turn and bolted away. It was sheer bad luck that he tripped over the tether, and even worse luck that he knocked the peg out of the ground. The horse immediately took off at speed, dragging the hapless Ansige a short distance until the rope finally pulled free.

Paama let out a shriek of genuine fear and dashed towards the nearest houses. 'Help! Help!' she shouted.

People came running, crying out, 'What is it? What's happening?'

'A terrible accident! The peacock went too close to our wild horse, and Ansige was trying to shoo him away when the horse broke free, trampled the poor peacock, and knocked Ansige down!' As she explained, Paama pointed wildly at Ansige, who was trying to pick himself up; the horse, who had slowed to a walk; and the bundle of feathers that had once been a proud peacock.

Some ran to help Ansige to his feet, others hastened to capture and secure the horse. The rest looked sadly at the limp remains of what had been the village mascot. 'Never mind, Paama,' they consoled her. 'It was just an accident. It could have been much worse.'

Ansige came limping to her side, rumpled and dazed. She took hold of his hand firmly. 'We must go tell the chief what happened. Say nothing. I will do all the talking,' she instructed him in a low voice.

The chief was out on his veranda enjoying the cool of the evening. He smiled at Paama and nodded to Ansige as Paama said her greetings and Ansige bowed stiffly, all too aware of the smudges of earth and bits of grass that still stained his face and clothing.

'Ansige, Ansige,' the chief muttered. 'Aren't you the son of Jeliah, daughter of Chief Darei of Hsete?'

'Yes, I am,' Ansige acknowledged, putting back his shoulders a bit and standing taller at this welcome piece of recognition.

'Yes,' smiled the chief, stroking his beard and looking very pleased with himself. 'I remember now. Did I not tell you he would make an excellent husband, Paama?'

Paama gasped suddenly to hide her indignation. 'Sir, I nearly forgot. We have some bad news to tell you. Makendha's peacock is dead! Ansige tried to save it, but it was trampled by my father's half-tamed horse.'

The chief sat up straight, dismayed. 'What misfortune! Why did it go so close to the horse?'

'It was so used to roaming about freely that it probably never realised it was in danger,' she said with complete if economical truth.

The chief stood, frowning. 'This is terrible. I will go immediately to see what the situation is.'

'A very good idea,' Paama agreed, and there was a strange hardness in her voice. 'One should never rely on a secondhand report for something so important.'

Later that night, after Ansige had been settled in at the lodge, Paama had time for herself. She went to the yard at the back of her parents' home and knelt down before a smooth river stone that had been set near the back gate. She eased it over, exposing a patch of smooth, hard earth. Dusting off her hands, she folded them in her lap and began to cry, carefully spilling her tears only where the stone had lain. After a few minutes, she squeezed out the last of her tears over the patch of bare earth, covered it back with the stone, and went inside.

3

ANSIGE AND THE UNEXPECTED HARVEST

SEMWE AND TASI WANTED TO comfort Paama, but it was very difficult to comfort someone who stayed so dry-eyed and unmoved. They compensated by buffering Paama from Neila's careless slights and self-centredness, and by praising the food on the breakfast table. At first Tasi had feared that she would be forced to invite Ansige to share the morning meal, but her husband reassured her that Ansige and his enormous appetite would not awaken until almost noon.

Still, the compliments fell flat. Talking about food reminded one of Ansige, and thinking of Ansige brought a tension to the atmosphere akin to a mental indigestion.

Semwe was the first to admit his thought. 'About your husband...' he began uneasily.

Paama stiffened, but the tremor was gone in a heartbeat and her shoulders slumped in the despair of acknowledgement. 'Yes, Father, I know. I know that Ansige has brought his huge, bottomless hunger into Makendha, and it must be satisfied or he will embarrass us all. But I do not know what I can prepare that will fill him. I have fallen out of the habit of planning meals for twenty.'

Semwe patted his daughter's arm while beside him Tasi made consoling noises. Neila, who was still oblivious to Paama's distress, continued eating and daydreaming and ignoring her family.

'I have a suggestion,' Semwe said. 'Why not send him a large basket of roasted corn? Roast enough for twenty men. That should keep him for the day. I really cannot see him getting through all of it.'

Paama smiled weakly, unconvinced. She might have forgotten how to cook for twenty, but there were many terrible memories of Ansige's eating still branded on her mind.

'I'll do that,' she replied. 'I'll go pick them right now so they'll be ready and roasted by the time Ansige wakes up.'

Paama went once more into the family lands and walked down the rows of maize, carrying a deep basket strapped to her back. While she picked, the growing heat of the sun beat down on her cloth-draped head until, wearied with her joyless task, she decided that she had picked enough. Then she carried her heavy load back to the yard behind their house, emptied the basket, and lit a fire under the large metal grill of the outdoor oven. As one batch of corn roasted, she wrapped it in palm leaves to keep in the heat and set it in the basket again. Roasting and packing, roasting and packing, she filled the basket up again.

'Now to get this to Ansige,' she said, hefting it onto her back once more.

When she got to the guest lodge, she expected to see Ansige, but she was told he was still sleeping. Secretly, she was relieved. She left the basket in the care of the other lodgers with strict instructions that it was to be given to Ansige the moment he awoke. Then she departed in gratitude, feeling lighter, and not only because of the lack of the heavy basket.

Ansige awoke, a delicious smell tickling his mind into full consciousness. He opened his door and saw the basket.

'What is that?' he exclaimed even as his nose confirmed the good news.

'Your wife brought it for you,' replied a passing fellow lodger.

A number of thoughts and emotions flashed through Ansige's mind. First he was very very glad that the delicious smell belonged to him and no-one else, but then he became instantly suspicious and annoyed. Imagine Paama leaving something like that out where anyone could have stolen it! In fact, perhaps the other lodgers had been picking at it all day while he slept. Perhaps they had stuffed the gaps with more palm leaves to make it look as full as ever.

'Ah ... thank you,' he said awkwardly, and dragged the basket into his room, shooting nervous glances about. What if more people saw his bounty and wanted to have a share in it?

He quickly washed and dressed, the smell teasing him all the while. Then he stuck his head out of his door and looked around furtively before sneaking out and trotting down the road with the basket on his back, heading to the only place he knew where he could eat alone and in peace—the fields.

He avoided the place of his previous crime—not consciously, perhaps, given that the crop fields were so much closer to the village than the pastures where the livestock grazed. He hopped over low vines of sweet potato and wove in and out of rows of maize until he was well in the centre, where he could not be disturbed. Then he began to eat.

It was delicious. Even the sight and sound of the maize rustling in the breeze above him seemed to add greater pleasure to his dining. For a while he revelled in it, but then something terrible happened. His arm plunged into the depths of the basket, and his hand scraped the bottom! A sinking sensation of loss made the comfortable, full feeling in his stomach lessen. He scrabbled through the discarded palm leaves around him in case he had missed one last corncob but eventually emerged empty-handed and depressed.

Imagine now Ansige in his nest of palm leaves, sitting dejectedly by an empty basket, all but pouting in his disappointment. An expression that would have been very familiar to Paama was present on his face: 'I am Constantly Mistreated and Abused.' He looked up to the heavens in entreaty, and his gaze was intercepted by the unusual sight of a single locust sitting on a corncob in one of the maize plants. It had peeled back the pale green leaves and was rubbing its forelegs in glee. Suddenly it became aware of Ansige's presence. It matched his unblinking stare for a brief moment and then seemed to shrug.

'Good corn,' it said conversationally, and reared back in preparation for the first grand bite.

Ansige roared. The locust took off in fright and spun off into the sky, never to be seen or heard or remembered again. Ansige snatched the corncob that it had sat on and snapped it off its stalk, brandishing his prize with another roar, this time of triumph.

Then, panting a little, he paused to consider the corncob in his hand.

After all, if he took a few, just enough to replace the ones that the others *stole* from him when the basket was outside his door, that wasn't stealing. That was just being fair.

Setting the basket on his back, he started to work. It was really amazing how industrious Ansige could be about anything that guaranteed a good feed at the end. Of course, since there wasn't any way for him to gauge how many had been taken from him, he kept picking, just to be sure. The sun was so hot in the early afternoon that he put aside his growing load and sought the shade of a breadfruit tree. Naturally that put ideas into his head, so he hooked down a number of the large green globes and built a small fire. After roasting many pieces on the point of a stick and eating his way through six of the starchy, football-sized breadfruits, you would have thought that he would forget all about corncobs, but all that happened was that he decided to nap for a while, just until the cool of the evening, when he could finish his harvesting in comfort.

Hours passed before he awoke again. The breadfruits had descended to the nether regions of his capacious stomach, and he was ready to top up again. Taking up his basket, he continued his previous work as twilight fell.

Meanwhile, Paama was growing uneasy. She had an instinct that told her that Ansige was heading for some kind of food-related trouble. She went on preparing dinner (the menu was greatly expanded as Ansige would be joining them at table) and tried to forget her vague fears, but when night fell and there was still no sign of him anywhere in the village, not even for a brief visit to lick the spoon, her sense of foreboding increased. Taking a torch, she went towards the fields, hoping he was not trying to capture another sheep.

Then she saw what looked like a squat, hunchbacked shadow lumbering towards the village. She began to call out.

'Ansige? Ansige is that you? Wait . . . be careful . . . you're too close to the . . . Watch out!'

There was a faint answering 'Aughhhhhhh!' sounding as if it were fading into the distance, and then an even fainter splash.

Paama ran. She skipped along the trail that led from the village to the fields, a trail which, on closer examination, did perhaps run entirely too close to the well for a stranger to tell the difference in the dark. She wondered how he had managed to topple over the low wall around the well that was supposed to keep out animals and small children. Then, when she shone the torch down the well, she almost shrieked. There was Ansige, bobbing in the midst of a huge mass of floating corncobs and fragments of basket.

'What are you doing?' she cried, not knowing whether to laugh or wail.

Ansige splashed, snorted, and spluttered. 'Don't act as if you don't know me! I ate the corn that you sent me, but since people *insist* on taking what isn't theirs, I had to fetch some more. And then a rock tripped me, and then the basket toppled me over, and then I was falling and—*stop laughing, you silly woman!* I could have been *killed!*'

Paama choked back her hysterical laughter. 'I'm sorry, Ansige. But look at you, stealing people's corn and talking about property rights! Now I have to get you out of this, in truth. You're far too heavy for me to pull up by myself. Wait—I'll be back soon.'

She rushed off, hardly attending to his grumble that he could hardly go anywhere now, could he? Then an idea came to her. Running as fast as she could, she went to a field of grazing cattle, untied them, and chased them into the cornfields. Only then did she dash back to the village. She began to raise the alarm, crying out for help as she ran along the streets. 'Help me! Help! Something terrible has happened! Ansige has fallen into the well!'

With such interesting news, people quickly came running out of their doors. 'In the well?' 'What happened?' 'How did he manage to do that?'

Paama gasped out her story. 'He saw cattle . . . they had got loose . . . they were trampling the young corn. He tried to chase them away, and he gathered up the ears that had been broken off. But when he tried to make his way back to the village in the dark, he stumbled off the trail and fell into the well!'

'Never mind, we'll get him out,' they reassured her, mistaking her panting breaths for distraught sobs.

With lights and ropes, they went to the well, and soon Ansige was hauled out onto dry land. Others rushed off to the cornfields and took the cattle back to their pasture. People clamoured around Ansige, trying to ask him his story of how such a thing had happened. Paama pushed forward quickly.

'Ansige, you must be in shock. People, please do not badger the poor man. He must get dry. He must change his clothes. He must have his dinner.'

'Dinner?' Ansige said plaintively.

All desire to talk about his ordeal vanished. He trotted obediently beside Paama towards her family's house.

4

ANSIGE LOSES HIS DIGNITY AND HIS HEAD

THE NEXT DAY, PAAMA WAS so miserable that even after she put her tears under the river stone, she could still feel the salt water sitting heavy on her heart. Her sister, who had finally seen Ansige at table, was at least more sympathetic than previously, but it wasn't enough. Her mother wore a look of suffering by proxy and guilt by association that gave Paama no comfort at all, at all, at all. Only her father gave her some hope. He was pondering the problem of Ansige so deeply that his brow was furrowed. Paama prayed that such strenuous mental effort would be rewarded with success.

She confided in him. 'Father, Ansige thinks that all the things that have happened to him are not because of his own foolishness, but because I am not taking proper care of him. What can I do?'

Semwe's frown fell away for a moment as he looked fondly at his daughter. 'Paama, there is very little that one can do when a foolish person chooses to think foolish things. But perhaps you could prepare for him a special dish, one of his favourites. You will satisfy both his ego and his appetite.'

Paama smiled. 'That is an excellent suggestion. I know what he would like best. Millet dumplings. I'll go start grinding the meal now.'

She set up her large mortar with its tall pestle in the court, the usual place to go to grind meal. After all, it was a job that had to be done singing, so that the rhythm could carry the motion of the pestle. As she worked and sang, passing villagers called out the familiar refrain in reply to her verses.

Beat him down, beat him down
then we can hold his wake
Maize for porridge, barley for beer
Millet for dumpling and cake

Beat him down, reaper
Beat him down, miller
Beat the grain man down

Scatter his bones in the field
Wait for the sun and the rain
Soon he shall rise up, ready for reaping
Ready for grinding again.

Raise him up, sun
Raise him up, rain
Raise the grain man up

Again Paama filled the mortar and ground the millet, and then filled and ground again. This was for Ansige, so naturally there would have to be a lot of it.

Mortar and pestle for drum
Trials and tears make a song
Look how we glad when a man rise up
But happier yet when he's down

Beat him down, brother
Beat him down, sister
Beat the grain man down

When the song had ended and the grinding was done, Paama's heart felt light at last. She caught sight of Ansige at the far edge of the court, looking at her as if his life depended on the contents of her mortar, and instead of being irritated at him, she felt sorry for him. Such an obsession with food could not be normal. Maybe he had a maw worm, a ravenous parasite living in his guts that ate the majority of the food he put into his body. Maybe he had a dislocation in his brain, so that instead of his feeling happiness, sorrow, or anger, his emotions were replaced by the sensation of hunger. She wished she could help him— not merely feed him to take away the hunger for a short while, but cure him so that food would never rule him again.

She mixed the millet with water, spices, and a touch of honey and cooked up a huge amount, platters full of dumplings, enough for twenty. When she brought them to Ansige, he was so ecstatic over this treat that she was able to go home, content and at peace, knowing that she could have a moment's well-deserved rest.

Ansige was indeed happy. To have food is always pleasant, but to have one's favourite dish, and to have it after watching it being prepared by the hands of someone who cares about you, that must surely be the greatest culinary delight. He ate and ate and ate until the sad moment arrived when he was holding the last dumpling in his hand. He popped it into his mouth and swallowed it down. Still hungry! Heaving a deep sigh, he looked around sadly and saw Paama's mortar still standing in the court.

'Good dumplings,' muttered a tiny voice by his foot.

He looked down, and there was a beetle, green and gold in the dusty brown soil of the court, worrying a large crumb of dumpling with its mandibles.

It looked up at him and, impossibly, winked. 'Bet you wish there was more where this came from, eh?'

Ansige's bottom lip pushed out in one of his variations on 'Woe is me!' Then he paused, struck by the beetle's words. Perhaps there *was* a bit of millet left at the bottom. There was only one way to find out. He went to the mortar and scraped a finger around the bottom, coming up with a tiny scoop of precious millet meal. Licking the finger clean, he again reached in and drew out another fingerful, but the small portions were more annoying than satisfying. There had to be a better way to get to the bottom of the mortar. Of course! He could put in his head and lick what he wanted straight from the sides and bottom.

It was one of his most brilliant ideas yet. He soon cleaned down the walls of the mortar and was heading for the remnants at the bottom when something disastrous happened. He could not get any closer! Frantically he extended his tongue as far as it could reach and strained to achieve the last few millimetres to his goal, but soon he had to admit defeat. He tried to pull his head out into the open.

Horrors! His ears, which had slid in so easily, refused to slide back up!

He tried a corkscrewing motion, turning his neck while his hands braced the edges of the mortar. If anything, it only made matters worse. Utterly chagrined, he scrambled blindly away to the side of a building and started to knock his wood-helmeted head against the wall.

Paama, he screamed in silent desperation, *if you come and get me out of this, I promise I will never take you for granted again!*

Paama sat up with a twitch. She had been relaxing, reclining, sipping coconut water and mulling over ways to convince Ansige to seek professional help for his problem. Then came this spasm, like a warning. It had been too quiet for too long. Ansige was not hanging around, begging for his between-meals snack. Something was wrong.

She ran to the fields, because that was where he had ended up during the previous two crises. No Ansige. She rushed back into the village and went towards the guest lodge.

Bup bup bup.

Paama wondered who could be pounding meal in such an odd fashion. Rather than the subdued, deep tone of wood on wood, it sounded like wood on stone.

Bup bup bup.

She came into the court and there was no-one there, but still there was this sound. There lay her own pestle, which she had left and forgotten after her morning's work...but where was the mortar? A knowledge of something, she knew not what, made her run to the alley by the guest lodge, the direction of the sound. What she saw there made her stop still for a moment in shock.

'Ansige? Ansige, is that you?' she asked incredulously.

'Don't act as if you don't know me!' he said, his voice muffled from the depths of the mortar and choked with tears of frustration. 'You had to go and leave a bit of millet at the bottom of the mortar, and my head got stuck when I tried to reach it. I can scarcely breathe!'

'Don't panic,' said Paama, a bit breathless herself with the strangeness of this scrape.

She ran to the court, muttering to herself, 'Now what do I do? I am running out of bright ideas.'

She began to yell. 'Help! Help! It is all my fault! It is all my fault!'

With such a good line, people could not resist coming to see who was blaming herself so freely. 'What is all your fault? What is the matter?'

'Ansige is stuck in my mortar! I told him he had a big head, and he said no, he didn't have a big head, and I said, "I bet you can't get it into my mortar. If I put my wedding ring into the mortar, could you get it out again using only your mouth?" And he said, "Just you wait, I'll show you," and then he put his head into my mortar, and now it's stuck and I'm to blame!'

The villagers looked at Ansige, listened to Paama's story, and burst out laughing. 'Never mind, Paama. We'll get him out somehow,' they said soothingly.

Perhaps it was unkind for them to laugh at him while he was in such a predicament, but no matter how you turned it about, who was the one at fault, the person who made the dare, or the person who took it up and came to grief? And wasn't this the third time in three days that they were running to rescue this man from some mishap?

Tasi and Semwe stepped out of the crowd and came up to their daughter. Tasi gave Paama a consoling hug and spoke quietly in her ear. 'A good story, but you are still wearing your wedding ring. Take it off and drop it on the other side of me, where no-one can see.'

Paama quickly obeyed while all eyes were still fixed on the strange sight of Ansige cowering in the alley with his head encased in a mortar. As the ring fell to the ground, Tasi immediately covered it with her foot, all the while patting Paama's shoulder comfortingly.

After some of the villagers had stopped laughing long enough to consider the problem, it was decided to use an axe to get Ansige out, and this had him so frantic with worry that he embarrassed himself further by whimpering and flinching. Finally they struck off only the very bottom of the mortar, quite a distance from his head, and then gently split the round open using a chisel and a crowbar. Every hammer and chop had been magnified a hundredfold by the wood pressing on his ears, and Ansige was quite traumatised when they finally got him loose.

Semwe took hold of his son-in-law with a grip that was sympathetic yet surprisingly firm. 'What a frightful experience! You must visit a doctor to ensure that there has been no permanent damage. Let me take you to the lodge and help you pack. The Makendha Infirmary is far too small to treat your case. We must get you to Ahani as soon as possible.'

Ansige followed Semwe without protest. In a bewilderingly brisk few minutes, he found that his belongings were packed, his bills settled, and a small crowd of villagers—some solicitous, some inquisitive, and some still frankly laughing at him—was escorting him to await the next omnibus to Ahani.

Paama watched him go, her arms folded and her lips folded as she listened to those who were quietly laughing and poking fun at Ansige. A wasp flew a time or two around her head, and certain ears would have heard it say:

'Look at him go! A fool to the last. No-one would think any less of you if you laughed at him, too, Paama. Go on, Paama! Beat the man down!'

Paama continued to stare at Ansige's retreating back. Behind her, half-hidden in the dust of the court, lay her discarded wedding ring. Tasi quickly stooped and picked it up, opening her mouth as if about to voice some reassurance, but Paama immediately turned away and walked homewards, not once looking at her parents, not once glancing up at the jeering insect.

Just outside the village, a pair of unseen observers exulted.

'Did you see that? She didn't hear it!'

'Or she heard it and ignored it.'

'Either way, she must indeed be the one to hold the Chaos Stick. They cannot influence her!'

'I'm glad you agree with me at last. Go arrange for it to be given to her as soon as possible.'

5

PAAMA RECEIVES AN UNUSUAL GIFT,
AND A LITTLE GIRL VISITS DREAMLAND

IN THE DAYS AFTER ANSIGE's departure, people were actually rather kind to Paama. When a woman leaves her husband and returns home for no apparent reason, there will be speculation, but after Ansige's display of gluttony-induced idiocy, no-one speculated any further. If anything, Paama was congratulated on having got rid of a burdensome spouse, and she was further respected because of her discretion and tact. Any other woman would have made a big fuss, or at the very least added her voice to the general mocking and ridiculing of the man and his deeds, but Paama seemed above all that.

'She will find a better husband some day,' was the verdict, and with that, the gossips moved on in search of more scandalous meat.

Paama, who had never cared very much what other people thought, still occasionally added to the saltwater lake under the river stone, but now there was more of the sweetness of relief than the bitterness of failure in her tears.

She accepted that her life with Ansige was over, so much so that when someone came knocking at the door claiming to bear a message from Ansige, her first reaction was bewilderment.

'A message? Why? Did he forget something when he left?'

The messenger was travelling light, with only a small courier's satchel over his shoulder. He did not look equipped to return with anything of significant size, so she discarded the thought even as she voiced it.

He bowed and said, 'Mister Ansige has sent me to ask you to return home.'

'Ask?' Paama repeated, stunned.

Still inclined in that respectful half bow, the messenger raised his downcast eyes and met the flash of not-quite-humour in Paama's eyes with a irreverent glint of his own.

'Do you have an answer for him, mistress?'

'Do I...oh...' Paama strangled for a moment as her words tripped over themselves while the messenger straightened and eyed her with compassion. She took hold of herself and spoke with strained calm. 'I am not going back. I am never going back, and he should know that. How dare he act as if...as if I didn't know him! Let him find another wife. I am no longer interested in the position,' she concluded with dignity.

The messenger bowed his head, a slow nod of acknowledgement. 'We expected as much. Well then, on to my second duty. The old servants remember how pleasant you made Mister Ansige's household for those who had to work there. You have been missed.'

He paused to dip his hand into his satchel and withdrew an object carefully wrapped in silk. 'We hope that you will accept from us this token of our thanks, and a remembrance of our sincere prayers that in the future you shall gain a better husband and a more blessed household.'

Paama took the narrow bundle, touched by the gift and the words that came with it. For courtesy, she unwrapped it there and then, so that he could carry back the tale of her delight and gratitude to the givers. When she saw what lay in the folds of ivory silk, she did not have to pretend to be awed. It was a stick such as one might find in any kitchen, the broad, flat kind made for turning meal to creamy smoothness. However, this one was made of ebony, and its handle was banded with etched gold. It was a trophy for her years of endurance with Ansige, and immediately she was very proud of it.

'Take it up, hold it,' insisted the messenger as she hesitantly extended her fingers over the gleaming finish of the handle.

Paama took the gift into her hand, and her eyes were so focused on admiring the workmanship that she missed the somewhat inappropriate expression of happy relief on the messenger's face.

'It is the most beautiful stirring stick I have ever seen,' she said.

'Yes,' the messenger murmured, constrained by the habit of truth. 'It is certainly a Stick for stirring things up.'

'I shall have to have it mounted on a plaque,' she mused aloud, turning it under the sunlight and wondering where she should hang it. 'Or perhaps a stand or rack of some sort might show it off better.'

'Why not hang it at your waist for now?' suggested the messenger. 'It has a loop for just that purpose.'

Paama stared at him. That was odd! Hanging it on her belt as if it were a guard's truncheon or a tradesman's tool. She started to tell him so, but the words evaporated. Shrugging at her own eccentricity, she did exactly as he said and hooked it onto her belt.

He smiled. 'Thank you. I will go take your answer back to Mister Ansige.'

Paama waved farewell as he trotted away from her front door. *'Thank you'? Why is he thanking me?* She watched him, slightly suspicious, to make sure that he did indeed head for the road leading out of the village. When he did just that, she laughed quietly at herself and her foolish thoughts and went back into the house.

Meanwhile, out of sight of the village, the messenger stepped quickly along the country trail until he was a day's journey out of Makendha. There was a sleeping heap huddled around the bole of a shak-shak tree, awaiting his return.

'Wake up,' he told it, giving it a friendly nudge with his foot. 'Go back and tell your Mister Ansige that Paama's words are, "Don't act as if I don't know you." She said some other things, too, but the general idea is that she's not coming back. Understood?'

The heap sat up and stretched. It was a man, the twin of the messenger in every way—features, figure, clothing, even the courier's satchel. He looked strangely fuzzy around the edges.

'Have I slept long?' he asked. It was the messenger's voice, too.

'Two days.'

The man was still stretching, making noises of pleased surprise. 'I cannot believe it. I have no stiffness, no pain . . .'

'Do you think I would steal two days of your life? To the world you slept for two days. To yourself mere minutes have passed since I left you.'

'What did she think of your gift?'

The faux messenger smiled. 'She likes it very much. When she learns what it is, she will love it even more. But no more questions. We will have an exchange—my memory of delivering the message to Paama for your memory of my existence. You promised,' he added as the man began to look downcast.

'I know. Will I see you again?' he asked hopefully.

'Me or someone like me,' came the cheerful reassurance. 'Now, hold still.'

He pressed a palm lightly on the man's forehead, and as he slowly faded into air, the real messenger grew solid and substantial. The man got to his feet, looked around with a slightly puzzled expression, and then set off with determination down the trail away from Makendha.

*

'Mission accomplished.' There was a certain amount of self-satisfaction in this communication.

'Are you back already?'

'I presented her with the Chaos Stick. Even as I speak, it is hanging from her belt.'

'Well done! And what else?'

'What . . . what else?'

'You *did* show her how to use it, of course?'

'I . . . I was supposed to show her how to use it? Oh. Dear. Um.'

'Exactly. You have to go back.'

The life of the undying is quite busy, either through dedication or desperation. The benevolent ones are the most diligent and the most overlooked, because they work with willing people and take their images as their shadows. The person who looks and in an instant reads your soul, the ordinary type who suddenly declares a profound and wise truth—I do not mean to take anything away from these people, for they are willing collaborators in a great work, but in many such cases they have lent their shadows for that pivotal moment.

Alas, there are others, not quite so benevolent, who entertain themselves by tormenting the lesser beings, namely humans. Co-operation is not a word that you will find in their lexicon, which is why they often find it simpler to snag a ride with a passing insect or any small creature whose brain can be easily overpowered.

Some are but tricksters, turning the tiniest of choices into a dire misstep or a trigger for catastrophe. Even very powerful ones, those who have learned to make their own shadows, sometimes do nothing more than tease and tweak fates a little, just for a good laugh. I am sure that the spider of Ahani was one of that sort, wreaking minor havoc in the form of his own whimsically-crafted shadow.

Others are more malicious, turning their powers to greater degradation than mere mockery. Many of those are powerful, for such work requires an amazing level of skill in its own warped way. Why, you may ask. Simple. Not one of them, no matter how powerful, can sway a body from its chosen course. The most they can do is help it along—grease the slope, as it were.

Carefully removing memories for generations still could not erase the collective awareness that there was *something* out there, going bump in the night or whatever. Thus several names had come to be attached to these immortal beings as they wrought both mystery and mischief through all countries, cultures, and centuries of humanity. Since the story is about Paama, we will use her country's name for them—the djombi.

This particular djombi, who was of the benevolent but not very powerful type, was experiencing a special kind of difficulty. For reasons that we cannot go into right now, a more powerful djombi was using his services. Unfortunately, his superior, who had long ago forged a shadow for herself, often appeared to forget the limitations of her weaker kin. By ending his errand and giving up his shadow too early, the junior was, in a manner of speaking, stranded, like a man who has neglected to ask the cab to wait for just a moment. He had to find another willing person to help him get back into Makendha so he could teach Paama the purpose of the Stick.

He was already too embarrassed by his earlier slip to ask directly for his superior's assistance, so he slunk to the fringes of Makendha and prayed for a small miracle.

His prayer was answered . . . very accurately, very precisely.

A little girl was playing at the edge of a pasture, dramatising some inner daydream with dance and song. She turned in midwhirl, caught sight of him, and tumbled over in surprise.

'What are you doing there?' she asked, peeking up through the grass stems.

'Waiting for someone to take me into the village,' he answered truthfully.

She narrowed her eyes and moved her head snakewise from side to side as if trying to look at a very tricky mirage. 'I can't see you very well. Why?'

He thought for a moment; truth is harder when one lacks the necessary vocabulary. 'I'm standing on the edge of the world. It makes things blurry.'

She got up and dusted herself off, apparently satisfied with that. 'All right. Good-bye.'

'Wait! Will you ... will you take me with you?'

She squinted at him again. 'Why?'

'I have to help someone discover something.' That was all he said, but for some things, tone and expression are more potent than vocabulary, even when you are a discorporate entity standing in the interstices of time and space.

She believed him. 'All right. Come.'

He stepped over the threshold and ran skipping towards her, a vaguely cloudy image gradually coalescing into an identical six-year-old girl.

She smiled then. Imaginary Twin was a familiar game. 'I'm Giana. What's your name?'

The djombi thought, shrugged, and replied, 'When I am without a shadow, I may be called Constancy-in-Adversity, though others who see me differently have sometimes named me Senseless-Resignation-to-Suffering. I am a small thing, as you can see, but my mother says I am quite powerful in my own way.'

Giana nodded. The names were too large and the concepts too weighty for her to grasp, but the last she could understand. Mothers tended to say things like that, usually just before sending you to the well to fetch water.

'Would you like to go play in dreamland until I come back?' the djombi asked her.

Her eyes lit up. 'Would I!'

He—or rather we must say 'she' now, as djombi take the gender of their shadows—took her by the hand and guided her gently to lie down on the ground.

'Now *you're* blurry,' she told the child softly as she tucked the long grass in a nest around her.

The child smiled back with sleepy sweetness, and then she was in dreamland.

The djombi stood up and looked over the fields. In the near distance there were other people tending to their animals in the pasture, all intent on their tasks, no-one noticing the strange momentary twinning of a little girl. One figure in particular now seemed familiar—a tall girl leading a cow by a long rope, a pail of milk balanced on her head.

'Giana, come here! I'm done with the milking,' she called over her shoulder with an older sister's offhand bossiness.

'Coming, Laira,' cried the djombi in her little girl voice, and she ran over the fields into Makendha.

6

THE DJOMBI BEGINS TO INSTRUCT PAAMA IN STICK SCIENCE

SIX-YEAR-OLD GIANA WAS BEING EXCEPTIONALLY naughty and no-one could figure out why. She would not play with her little friends, she often ran off when she should have been helping in the kitchen or fetching water, and, strangest of all, when her mother gave her a lash with the switch for her laziness, instead of crying as she would normally do, she gave her mother such a reproachful and annoyed look that the poor woman dropped the switch guiltily and edged away, feeling extremely unnerved.

Giana's Gran, who had become perceptive through years of experience, told them to leave the child alone. She said that something had got into Giana's head and they would have to wait until it went back out again. Giana gave the old lady a big hug and got a wink in return, but her older siblings muttered about how spoiled she was, and how *they* would never have gotten away with such behaviour when they were younger.

There was little connection between Giana's family and Paama's, so Giana was forced to go looking for Paama herself. She wasted an entire day trying to see her and speak to her, either out in the fields or in the court, but each time there were too many people around, or someone who could not be safely ignored was telling her to run along.

In the meantime, there were tantalising glimpses of the potential

49

of Paama's new gift. Giana was amazed. How could people miss the way Paama's feet stirred the dust of the trails into delicate, artistic swirls? How could they fail to notice that the long grass of the pastures combed itself into neat order when she breezed past it? One thing they did see, and that immediately, was that her skill in the kitchen had reached the level of pure magic. The scents that wafted from the house of Paama's parents made many a body slow down as they passed and break into bemused smiles of sheer bliss.

All this in one day? the djombi thought with a mixture of worry and pride. *I must talk to her as soon as possible!*

Fortunately, the next morning she found Paama washing clothes by the river. This was usually a communal task, with many women talking and singing together, but today Paama was by herself.

Giana decided to waste no time. She marched straight over to Paama and said, 'Paama, what is that thing on your belt for?'

Paama stopped her work and stared at the little girl. 'Small children must not be so informal with their elders. I am sure you have been taught better than that.'

Of course. Giana grimaced in embarrassment and tried again. 'Aunty Paama, what is that thing on your belt used for?'

Paama smiled mysteriously and went back to slapping the wet cloth against the smooth stones. 'It is for reminding me that good can come out of the worst of situations.'

Giana was startled and pleased. Perhaps Paama did not have as far to go as she had feared. 'Does it work for other people, too?'

Paama appeared to consider this seriously for a moment, and then she shrugged. 'I don't see why it would. Perhaps they have their own reminders. But, child, why are you wandering around near the river by yourself? Does your mother know you are out?'

Giana looked around for an excuse, feeling keenly the limitations of her chosen shadow.

'*They* come down to the river all the time,' she said at last.

She pointed downstream to where three boys were playing a variation of King of the Castle. They were wrestling, barebacked and barefooted, on a large, mossy rock, each trying to push the other into the water.

Paama gave them a glance. 'And why should you try to copy them? Big boys don't play like little girls, and what they are doing is far too dangerous for you to even think about.'

'It looks as if it might be too dangerous for them, too,' said Giana calmly, still looking down the river.

'They can all swim,' Paama said with a dismissive shrug.

She continued swinging the wet cloth and slapping it down. Fine droplets of water spun off from the fabric as it arced through the air, catching the sunlight and scattering tiny rainbows around her. Giana's attention was caught by the display. With the Chaos Stick at her belt, Paama was unconsciously selecting the most appealing options that chance had available. There were uncanny patterns in the water and the light, patterns that appeared to be unnatural and contrived but were merely very very rare, requiring just the right combination of angles for sun, water, and wind.

'She truly is a natural,' sighed Giana to herself while Paama slapped and scrubbed at the clothes in a manner that would have seemed completely mundane and ordinary to the untutored eye.

'About the Stick,' she began again, wondering how to go about explaining the science behind the Stick to one of Paama's limited education.

There was a sudden commotion. One of the boys had tumbled into the water and was bawling loudly. The little girl jumped at the sound and forgot the rest of her sentence.

'They can all swim,' Paama repeated, not even bothering to look up.

'Even with a broken wrist?' Giana wondered aloud.

Paama jumped up to stare at the drama downriver. One boy remained standing on the rock, pointing at his friends and yelling. Another boy was swimming towards the unfortunate one, who floundered and splashed while clutching his right hand in his left. Panicked with pain, he lashed out with his feet at the boy who was trying to save him, catching him a solid blow that pushed him off and spun him away.

'No. He'll drown them both,' Paama breathed. She dropped the washing and began to run down the river bank.

'Paama! You can't reach them in time! Use the Stick instead!' Giana called out, running after her.

'What stick?' Paama shouted back.

Giana began to babble in her haste to take advantage of this unplanned situation. She tried to explain about the different possibilities in the universe, about the chance that seems improbable but that, once it is possible, might still happen. And what if there were a type of focus or control for the quantum fluctuations that determine whether a situation is Go or No Go? One could use it to select the unlikely and encourage the serendipitous. One who had the knack of getting the best out of bad situations. One like Paama.

'What? What?' Paama yelled distractedly.

Giana was ready to scream herself, but she was too out of breath from making her short legs keep up with Paama's.

'Just use the Stick!' she gasped.

'You're right. We do need a stick, but there isn't one big enough!' Paama said, looking around in desperation.

They had drawn level with the boys in the water. Paama danced sideways along the bank, keeping in line with them and in pace with the slow current, but hesitant to risk diving in and struggling to bring one wildly flailing body to land.

'If only there were a branch or snag that they could hold on to,' she wailed.

There are any number of trees that grow on the banks of rivers, and it is in the nature of trees to occasionally lose a limb to age and decay. Time and wind cooperated to bring to breaking strain the dying branch of an overhanging tree several metres downstream. The branch tore free with an awful creaking and cracking and fell with a sloshing splash into the river, immediately lodging firmly against the rocks. The boys drifted into it and clung fast. Giana stopped short, stunned by Paama's words and their effect.

'Thank God,' gasped Paama.

Then the third boy rushed up and helped Paama drag the stricken youngster out of the water. His would-be rescuer, who was still curled over from that hard kick, was able to pull himself out onto the bank without help. Giana stood for a moment, hands limp at her sides with relief, watching as they sat or sprawled on the grass and fussed over the injured boy. He was sobbing and coughing from the pain in his wrist and the water he had swallowed while screaming, but he was too loud to be anything but alive. She came up to them, put her arms akimbo, and looked down at them critically.

'Well, I suppose that wasn't too bad, though it was a bit . . . much. A more subtle use of the currents, perhaps, or—'

'Shut up,' said the uninjured boy, getting up and shoving roughly at her shoulder.

She staggered back and stared at him, appalled at such rudeness.

'Stop that,' Paama snapped. 'Both of you, make yourselves useful and go up to the village and get help.'

The boy trotted off immediately. Paama turned her full attention to Giana. She seemed increasingly irritable now that the crisis was over.

'And you, little girl, don't come back down to the river unless your mother is with you. Can you imagine if it had been you in the water? You might not have been so lucky.'

'But—'

'Don't answer back. Do you want me to tell your mother what a disobedient little girl you are? Now go!'

Giana went.

The evening's debriefing was depressingly short.

'How are the lessons going?'

'I don't mean to be difficult, but explain to me again why Paama needs to be taught how to use the Stick when she seems to be playing it so well by sheer instinct.'

'Don't make me mention any names.'

There was a contrite silence, and then, 'I know, I know. I'm a little stressed. I have had to face some challenges because of the nature of my chosen shadow.'

'Be direct. Remember, you don't have to take away her memories. But no-one else must find out.'

'I know,' muttered the junior djombi morosely. 'I know.'

The morning after, Paama was sweeping her doorstep when she looked up and saw the little girl from the river. She was walking alone, despondently kicking at dust with her bare toes. Paama's heart softened.

'Child, come here,' she called.

The girl came up to her and looked up into her face with a surprisingly anxious expression. Paama remembered how many times she had scolded her the day before and was instantly contrite.

'The boys will be all right. They have been warned not to play in the river again until they are older. So, you see it's not just you.'

The girl didn't seem satisfied by this news. She said sorrowfully, 'I didn't go down to the river to play. I went to see *you.*'

Paama was surprised and touched by the earnestness in the child's tone but did not know how to respond to it. Then she found something to say.

'I have just finished baking small cakes. Would you like to come in and have some?'

The small face lit up. 'Yes, thank you!'

When they got inside, she seemed slightly dismayed that Paama's sister and mother were also in the kitchen, but after a few of the cakes were inside her, she was much more cheerful.

'May I come back and see you tomorrow?' she asked Paama with the directness of innocence.

'Yes, once your mother agrees,' Paama said.

'She will now that Gran has spoken to her. I think that mothers worry far too much about their children, don't you? It's very stifling.'

Paama raised her eyebrows, but Tasi and Neila looked at each other, smiled, and shook their heads fondly. The child was so precocious—an endearing trait at six, but Paama silently hoped that Giana's mother would shake it out of her before six more years were past.

7

A SENIOR DJOMBI MISSES SOMETHING DEAR TO HIM

WE ARE GOING TO LEAVE Paama and Giana for a while, because there are other things happening elsewhere that we should examine now lest they surprise us later on.

Picture a hall. The roof is vaulted timber with winged creatures carved into the beams that arch overhead. It is like looking into the bottom of a boat, most likely the Ark, given the presence of the creatures, and yet perhaps not, since no such beasts ever survived the Flood. The floor is cold stone, dark and light, like an oversized chessboard. There are pillars, also of stone, that lend a solid, reassuring support to the descending arc of the roof. The stone of the pillars glitters faintly, as if hewn of some unpolished gem.

Beyond the pillars are more pillars, presumably supporting similar roof structures, a whole fleet of upturned boats to the right and to the left of this main enclosure. If there are walls, I cannot see them to give you any report of them.

It is supposed to be majestic, the hall of a high lord. Instead, it is empty, sterile, and cold, speaking not of present pomp, but of ultimate futility. It proclaims that all is vanity.

There is a throne. The throne is unoccupied.

Now that you have that scene firmly in your heads, I can bring in the villain.

No, Ansige was not the villain of the story. He was the joker, the momentary hindrance, the test of character for Paama's growth and learning. He was the unfortunate, but not the villain. You may have felt sorry for Ansige, you may have laughed at Ansige, but you will not laugh at this person.

I have mentioned previously the three different categories of undying ones. Never assume that these categories represent boundaries that are never crossed or lines that cannot be redrawn. It is not the known danger that we most fear, the shark that patrols the bay, the lion that rules the savannah. It is the betrayal of what we trust and hold close to our hearts that is our undoing: the captain who staves in the boat, the king who sells his subjects into slavery, the child who murders the parent.

The djombi are like the human creatures they meddle with, apt either to great evil or great good, and sometimes they switch sides.

This one was the unknown danger. He had switched sides. He had started with benevolence, with the belief that there is a fine potential in humankind waiting only to be tapped. He now viewed the whole stinking breed as a pest and a plague. We may view him as a villain, but he would see us as cockroaches.

He had made for himself a very striking shadow. During his days of borrowing shadows, he had noted how responsive the human creature could be to a messenger clothed in classic beauty. As he became more powerful, he was careful at first, making his image handsome enough, but not too handsome to excite envy, and always being careful to add that slight signature difference that underlined his alien nature. Then he did less of walking with the creatures and more of observing and influencing from a distance, and he discovered that a form closer to the ideal obtained better results for his brief visitations. Even then, if he had only realised it, he had started to slip, caring less and less about the people he was supposed to be helping, and focusing much more on the respect and admiration that he felt was his due right as a superior being. When at last he became cynical, he set his form and features to the zenith of perfection, and then, instead of choosing a subtle mark, he made his skin deep indigo—a stark and utter setting apart that provoked as much of horror as of awe, mingled as it was with that unearthly beauty.

Clothed in white linen like a chief, he walked the broad aisle of his hall. There was no smile on his face, and it looked as if there had not been one in some time. Occasionally, a muscle by his jaw twitched as if he chewed on bitter and painful thoughts, but his walk was slow and peaceful. Then he passed a pillar, and the control was abruptly abandoned. He lashed out at the innocent stone, striking a shard of square-faceted crystal from the smooth side of the pillar. The hall shivered at the blow.

He was angry, he was more than angry, he kept telling himself how angry he was, but the truth was that he was ashamed. He had not had reason to question himself and his deeds for a very long time, but now others had dared to judge him and, apparently, find him wanting. They had taken away that aspect of his power of which he was most proud, his ability to balance the forces of chaos.

He had other powers, that was true, more than enough to go his own way and do his own will, but he had never really thought of himself as having crossed over the line until this happened. Even if he wasn't working with them anymore, all he had asked was for the opportunity to continue more or less as before. He would not stop them in their foolish attempts to assist humankind, and they, he had hoped, would respect his changed opinions and leave him to his entertainments. Instead, they had effected this near-demotion, stripping him of authority and rejecting his neutrally framed allegiance to his misguided siblings.

No. He would not stand for this. The power of chaos was his. He was the only one who could control it, and he was going to take it back.

Now resolved, he snapped his fingers and dissolved the royal hall. It was just another fleeting amusement, designed to alleviate the aching boredom of purposelessness that he felt so often of late. Then he let himself fall from empty air, diving from an impossible height for many long seconds until he pierced the surface of the ocean, dragging innumerable trails of bubbled air after him. Down he went, deep, deep down, with all the momentum that the high fall had provided. The water turned quickly from clear aquamarine to a dark, murky green-blue, then a thick, smoky darkness proclaimed that the light had failed to beat this far through the layers of liquid.

Yet there *was* light. An eerie, greenish glow loomed ahead.

'Greetings, Lord.'

Remember that the djombi custom is to have no names. How did this one manage to snag for himself such a noble title?

'Greetings, King of Dark Waters. I am looking for a focus of chaos. Have you seen anything unusual?'

The shadowy King gurgled and swished a lazy tentacle. 'I am the most unusual thing in these waters, and that is as it should be. Ask another. We want no trouble here.'

His words were disquieting. Had they warned the King about him? Still, no-one could lie to him; if the King said chaos was not here, it was not. He bade him a polite but cold farewell and repeated his long dive in reverse, shooting up and out of the water with such force that he went several metres into the air.

'Are you looking for me?' came a sly voice.

The undying one spun gracefully and came to float alongside the speaker. 'I am, and I have found you. My question is, have *you* found chaos?'

The Commander of Bright Winds flapped his wingtips with a flair that was almost apologetic. 'My Lord, would I go looking for chaos? We have enough to do here to survive without dabbling in affairs too grand for us. Ask someone else.'

Only one element of the living remained, but the thought of walking the Earth again made him pause and shiver fastidiously, as if in anticipation of dirt and grime. He braced himself and set his feet to ground. It was not hard to find her; she rarely left her savannah these days. Her right foreleg stamped, sounding the earth like a hollow drum, and her right eye looked at him with an unfriendly glitter. Djombi or not, he instinctively put himself out of range of the sweep of her trunk. Clearly the Queen of Ever-Changing Lands was not pleased to see him. He asked his question with uncharacteristic diffidence.

'Do I not have enough trouble with your kind taking advantage of the insects and inciting the humans to greater and greater damage?' she blared in reply. 'Of course I have seen chaos. Where the focus of it might be, I cannot tell you. Ask one of your own.'

He was slightly perturbed that she had so quickly categorised him as one of the aimless troublemakers, but he was too worried about his lost power to dwell on that for long. Swallowing his pride, he went to a well-known djombi, the godfather of the troublemakers.

'Strange seeing you here, Lord.'

It was the spider of Ahani, and when he said 'Lord', he took care to make it sound like a poorly delivered joke.

'You know what I am looking for. Do not trifle with me.' He was beginning to lose his temper.

'I? Trifle? I assure you, I am the one who has been hard done by. What is this new experiment you and your people are trying?'

'Not "my people". Not before and not now. And I do not know what you are talking about.'

'I am referring to this human who now wields the power of the djombi.'

He took a deep breath. This surely was news of a most chaotic type, unravelling the natural order of things. It was as if someone had started supplying the ants with automatic weaponry. 'No human can manage the power of the djombi. They lack the most basic of skills. They are not even designed for it. Someone has been tricking you, O Trickster.'

The spider only smiled. 'I hear that she is a natural with the Chaos Stick.'

A burning hatred poured over his veneer of calm like flame spreading on an oil slick. To take away his power so cavalierly, and then to give it to a human? Was that not the insult that crowned the injury? He was appalled at their lack of decency. Still, they didn't call this one the Trickster for nothing. He struggled with himself, hid his emotion, and continued.

'Let us imagine for a moment that I believe you. Where is this human to be found, and what marvels has it worked?'

The spider understood him in an instant. 'I have no more to say to you. Give a spider a bad name and let him hang . . . you know I cannot lie to you, but you will never trust my words. Go to Makendha and see for yourself, and forget that I said anything about the situation. In fact, I wash my hands of the whole business.'

With a beautifully feigned air of offended injury, the spider stalked away.

The indigo lord returned briefly, recreated his hall with a careless thought, and began to angrily pace its floors. Its emptiness was an unbearably painful mockery, mirroring the aching gap left by the extracted power. He refused to beg the djombi to return his power, and none of the troublemakers were likely to want to help him. By choice, he had always worked alone. He had no allies, no juniors to send to do his bidding.

There was only one option. He would have to go to Makendha himself, and get his power back.

8

THE INDIGO LORD SPIES ON THE CITIZENS OF MAKENDHA

TO WALK BOLDLY INTO MAKENDHA would not be prudent. At the very least, the exercise demanded some initial reconnaissance. The indigo lord reluctantly decided to take up that despised practice: stealing the shadow of an insect. However, to save time and emphasise his superior ability, he took not one but several at once—honeybees, dragonflies and a handful of ladybirds. Shadowing multiple insects of multiple species was a pleasurable challenge, one that occupied his mind so that there was little energy left for fretting and fuming.

His dragonflies patrolled the river and the wells and the ponds where the livestock were watered. The ladybirds bore the protection of superstition, for they were considered lucky, so he allowed them to settle on people's clothing and travel with them into houses where they could overhear all the latest gossip. The honeybees flew in and out everywhere, but were often distracted by flower gardens and kitchens. He managed them all with the fine skill of an orchestral conductor, scanning the news they found for information that would help him regain his power.

It became clear to him very quickly that the people of Makendha had no inkling of what was in their midst. He began to worry that perhaps the spider had, after all, sent him to scramble uselessly on a fruitless errand. Then he consoled himself. There was no way that any djombi could sense his presence in Makendha, with his power so widely diffused into such weak shadows. Also, why assume that the person who held the chaos power was indeed as proficient as the spider claimed?

Chaos was a far subtler force than most people realised. It would be so easy to sense if it threw off thunderbolts or sent barely sensed thrummings through the fabric of reality, but it was nothing more than the possible made probable. It did not break or bend any laws of nature or tip the balance of the universe. How would a mere human understand how to manipulate it? They would end up thinking they were merely lucky, or blessed.

Finding someone who held an unused or little-used focus of chaos was akin to the unenviable task of trying to find a needle in a haystack. He tried to see if there was anyone who stood out from the crowd. He looked for the village herb woman, he scrutinised the chief, he examined the local priest. They were all within the ordinary mould, with ordinary events surrounding them. Then he spied for a while on the strongest hunters, the most successful farmers, the wealthiest merchants. None of them had come by their fortunes recently and serendipitously. Finally, growing bored at last and ready to give up, he looked at the women of Makendha, to see who was the most power-ful matriarch.

It took a bit of a stretch of the imagination, but the only person who remotely stood out was Tasi.

It made sense in a way. She was not a woman who stood out for her own merits, and yet her husband was prosperous enough and respected among the village elders, her daughters were of good repute, and her kitchen drew ordinary passersby like honey draws sugar ants. As he pieced together the gossip, he became even more certain. Her older daughter had married a man considered foolish even by human standards. When he came to Makendha to see his estranged wife, bizarre accidents were the result. He had left the village without her, and with very little of his dignity. Yes, ridicule was the weapon of the quiet woman.

His insects focused their attention on Tasi's household. Not only the kitchen attracted visitors. The younger daughter, who was still single, had several strings of admirers. It seemed as if Tasi was employing a very strict screening process, however. Before the suitors were given any opportunity at conversation with the object of their desire, they had to sit through a detailed interview with Tasi and her older daughter. Few made it past this first, intimidating obstacle, and those who did endured the chaperoned visits for interminable weeks after that. There were compensations; the food of Tasi's kitchen was truly delightful by all accounts. However, no one had as yet gained the prize.

Still, he needed confirmation. These were only hints, and he was not about to make a fool of himself for the Trickster to gloat over him. Then, at last, he found it. A junior, cunningly hidden in the shadow of a child, had insinuated itself into Tasi's household!

He instantly grew cautious. Sending away all but two of his shadows, he flew a bee in at the kitchen window and walked a ladybird over the threshold of the back door.

'Why don't you simply show me how to use it?' murmured a woman's voice.

'I would rather not even touch it,' a child whispered back.

His shadows were poorly positioned for a clear sight of the speakers. The djombi was easily identified by its piping child's voice, but the voice of the other could have been either of Tasi's daughters for all he could tell. He turned the bee and flew to the other side of the room so that he could see the faces . . .

Splat.

There was a sudden loss of aerial vision. His bee had been swatted.

'Neila! Why did you do that?'

'I hate bees. They look like they're waiting to sting you for no good reason.'

'That's wasps, Neila! You like honey, don't you? Then let the bees live!'

Those two voices were almost identical. He was growing confused. Determinedly, he set his ladybird crawling up a wall for a better line of sight. When he turned it about to look down at the room, he saw the two daughters, and the child-shadow. The child was looking up at his ladybird with an expression of cold suspicion, and he realised that he had spent too much time getting into position.

'Would you kill that ladybird?' it said to Neila, continuing to look meaningfully at the bright red beetle.

'Don't be silly. No-one would kill a ladybird. What would happen to all my luck if I did a thing like that?'

A pot on the stove rattled. The older daughter was stirring the contents and examining them closely.

'The syrup is ready,' she announced, bringing the steaming pot to the table and setting it on a round of stone.

A sheet of chilled metal was also on the table. She took out a generous dollop of syrup and handed the spoon to the child, who then carefully dribbled strings of syrup onto the cold metal. There was more confirmation if he needed it—the strings tumbled into weird spirals and highly specific knots, a sure sign of chaos if one knew what to look for.

... But the djombi wasn't doing it, at least not if he understood that first exchange correctly. Tasi wasn't in the room, so it wasn't her ...

The two sisters sat with heads close together, watching the liquid as it curled into its patterns and peeling it off when it solidified.

It had to be one of them.

He believed it must be the younger. A woman cautious of her

luck, but contemptuous of the lives of bees, with half the men in the village and some from out of it beating down her door, yet perhaps close enough to her sister to do her the favour of ridding her of the encumbrance of a foolish husband ... yes, it was very likely.

He had no idea how biased he had become. He saw Neila's beauty, her casual cruelty, and her boredom, and he saw himself. Naturally he believed her to be the one gifted with his stolen power.

Careful not to attract attention, he let the ladybird fly away home. He no longer needed it. He felt so pleased with himself that instead of conjuring the hall, he relaxed and imagined himself a warm sunny pasture to lie in while he plotted out the recovery of his power. There was still the problem of where the focus was located. Humans did not hold such power within themselves easily; they had a deep-seated need for symbols, talismans, and representations. Somewhere in that house was the symbol of the force of chaos, and unless he took that with him, he could not take back the power.

That junior djombi would be on the alert now. It would look out for insects and guard its words from being overheard, and warn the women to guard theirs too. It would double its efforts to teach Neila how to use her new gift effectively. He had little time if he hoped to avoid an unseemly battle with juniors and inferiors.

He remembered Neila's offhand tones after she spoke of killing the bee. She was interesting, in a mundane and wholly human kind of way. Perhaps he could convince her to give up his power without a struggle. She looked like a woman who could be bribed. In fact, she looked like a woman who could be flattered. If he came to her as a suitor, with enough wealth and beauty to dazzle her, would she even notice that her power over chaos was no more when she saw all the apparent luck around her?

True, it had been a while since he walked the earth in a human role, but there were precedents. It might be the easiest way to get back his power. Who knows what terrible things they had said to her about him? Better that he try honey and temptation to reach his goals rather than attempt to use force, which might only justify any misconceptions already given.

It sounded like logical reasoning, but he was biased again. He secretly wanted to punish Neila. She would choose him as her husband, but after he got what he wanted, he would desert her. He wanted to humble her, to make her feel as if she was winning and then show her the face of her defeat when she was a mere hair's breadth from the pinnacle. She dared to take the power of a senior djombi, then let her defend herself!

Remember what we mentioned to you before. This is a dangerous person. He enjoys lulling the prey into a feeling of safety before killing it. That instant of betrayal, that twist of perception when one realises that one's entire universe is founded on a lie—that is the moment that acts on his boredom as splendidly as champagne on a jaded palate.

9

A STRANGER IS COMING TO MAKENDHA

THOSE WHO LIVE IN MAKENDHA say that Ahani is the place where con men hold their conventions. They may be right—certainly it must have had some seedy flair to attract the regular attention of a djombi like the Trickster. Another claim made about Ahani is that a man can make something of himself there. That also had some grains of truth. Certainly it was not kind to women seeking their fortunes—not entirely baseless is the belief, widespread in Makendha and beyond, that women rule the villages but men rule the towns. As for making something of oneself, the question remains, what would that something be?

The indigo lord was going to Ahani to make an identity and a reputation for himself. Just because he considered them vermin didn't mean he lacked awareness of how humans operated. As individuals they were puny, but as hives their communication networks had power. There was no way he could impress in Makendha if no-one had ever heard of him in any of the larger cities.

He went to a stash of gold which he had put away—the legacy of an adventure in more innocent days. Perhaps I will tell you about it later, if we have the time. He had never expected to use it for himself, but that was the nature of chaos; its effects spanned time in ways that were not always immediately discernible, not even by beings outside of time.

He found a modest but highly reputable guest house in Ahani, one where his lack of goods would not be commented on. His first step was to hire a man of discretion. The way that he did this was to conduct the interviews in his usual shadow. Those who flinched at the strange colour of his skin, or whose eyes asked questions, did not pass. Finally, he selected a man by the name of Bini, whose calm eyes and unruffled demeanour spoke of vast pools of patience and a truly inhuman lack of curiosity. His only concerns were his duties and his pay, and once assured that the former were legal and the latter significant, he had nothing more to say.

Except one other thing.

'May I ask m'lord's name or title, so that I might know who has hired me and for whom I will be hiring?'

It was a fair request. The indigo lord had an answer waiting. 'You may call me Taran.'

'Taran' was not a common name. It meant 'star' in the local language. Bini merely nodded, taking the strangeness of the name and dropping it into the bottomless pit of his nonchalance.

Having secured his majordomo, Taran, as we may now call him, assigned to him all the hiring of the lesser servants and the acquisition of goods. Bini proved to be the same as all the rest, but when he returned with his first and only set of doctored receipts, Taran gave him a moment to feel comfortable and then struck him down with the truth, that truly formidable axe against which little can stand. Bini deserved credit; rather than bluster or try to cover up his gaffe, he said quietly that the receipts appeared to be misleading and he would return in a while with the correct figures. After that, there was no more trouble with Bini, though Taran kept a changing guard of insects near him—a beetle one day, an ant the next—just to be sure.

Taran showed his face once to Bini during the interview; after that he covered himself entirely, robes, gloves, boots, and veiled headdress with only his eyes glinting beyond a rectangle of mesh. He looked like a desert prince travelling incognito. He offered no explanation for his sudden change in garb. As a human, Bini would come up with his own speculations . . . then again, as Bini he would probably not care.

I myself have wondered why Taran did not simply change his shadow to blend into his environment. I suspect—and this is subject to correction—that such large-scale changes to one's own shadow were performed infrequently. It may be that the act of shadowcrafting not only requires great effort, but also creates a ripple that can be sensed by like beings. For all his pride, Taran was not above using stealth in order to gain the advantage. Or maybe it was indeed pride that made him cover himself so that he would not be soiled by human touch, not even by their eyes resting on his features. I do not know.

The underlings hired by Bini did speculate. He overheard one declaring that he was probably hiding ghastly scars from a severe burning, and another guessing that the mark of pestilence was what caused him to hide his skin. The most inventive hypothesis thus far was that he was terribly sensitive to heat and light due to albinism, which would also explain the strange purplish hue of his eyes that could be detected even through the mesh.

Taran had not forgotten his plan. He ensured that his clothes were tailored to fit him well so that all could see that his shadow was healthy, excellently proportioned, and lacking in deformation of any kind. He correctly assumed that his wealth would provide sufficient attraction to counter the unseen but imagined flaws. Beautiful women like Neila are not interested in competitors. Without a doubt she would prefer a man with the means to display her beauty to its best advantage over a man whose beauty rivalled hers.

When all was made ready and his staff and stores fully equipped, Taran made one more request of Bini. Before their departure, he wished to hire a poet. This was in keeping with the strange scruples of his fallen state. Like all his kind, he was incapable of lying, but he had too much pride remaining to twist truth in the manner of tricksters. Hiring a man to lie for him was the perfect compromise. Besides, for poets it wasn't lying, it was art.

Back in Makendha, Paama was adjusting to the fact that little Giana was not what she seemed. She saw her often, at least once a day, when fetching water or tending to the animals or washing clothes. Otherwise they met in the kitchen, but there they had to be careful of Neila and Tasi stumbling in on a strange conversation filled with strange words. In spite of that, it seemed to be Giana's favourite place . . . or perhaps she was merely enjoying the sweet tooth of childhood amid Paama's pastries and sweets.

'Why should it come to me?' had been Paama's first real question, the question that signalled her acceptance that this was not a dream or a joke. 'This is a powerful thing, the way you describe it. Why should any human being have such power?'

'I do not know,' Giana replied softly, as if ashamed to admit it. 'I only know that I was told to give it to you, and that once you had it, you began to use it as if it were a lost part of yourself. There may be a reason, but it is beyond my knowledge.'

Paama looked at her, itching to ask more questions, but these were the ones she dared not have answered, so she wisely did not ask them.

'What am I supposed to do with it?' she asked instead.

'For now? Learn it, understand it so that it becomes more than instinct. A stranger is coming to Makendha, Paama. He is nearby, making his preparations. I have already seen his spies. You must be strong against him, for he wants to take back the power that was once his.'

'Then why did you waste time teaching me to spin five hundred different configurations of sugar spirals?' Paama scolded her, alarmed at this news. 'You should have been showing me how to fight him!'

'Set your mind at ease, Paama. It is not power that you should be concerned about. Power you already have. I have been teaching you control. Plus, they were delicious. Now I have told you all that I can, all that you need to know. Remember it well, because I cannot stay with you any longer.'

'Where are you going?' asked Paama, forgetting for a moment and wondering why she had not heard of Giana's family leaving Makendha.

'Giana must come back. It has been almost seven days, and that is the limit for a child. I mustn't abuse her generosity.'

'Where is Giana?' Paama asked, this time with an edge of apprehensiveness in her voice.

'Come and see.'

Paama walked with the djombi into the pasture and saw the faint, sleeping shape of another Giana. It was the final feather to tip the balance of her teetering belief-disbelief. She felt the ground falling out from under her feet.

'You cannot leave me by myself! Will I never see you again?'

'You may see me, or not, but I will definitely see you. Don't be afraid, Paama. But be cautious. Trust your instincts. Now, let me speak to Giana alone.'

Paama turned away, shivering under the high, hot sun. She stood looking back at the village and was very startled when a small hand tugged at her belt.

'I'm ready to go back now,' said that familiar voice, but a subtle difference told Paama who it was who now lived beneath the child's skin.

Paama looked beyond Giana, but the pasture was empty. She

extended cold fingers and took the child's hand. They walked slowly back to Makendha in a silence mildly tinged with the sorrow of loss.

Both the gift of the Stick and the djombi's words meant something quite significant to Paama. Even before Ansige had arrived, she had wondered to herself how much longer she should stay with her parents. Now she felt she had even more reason to try to order her life—a life outside of Makendha. She wanted to travel. A good cook could find work anywhere, in a household, on a ship, in a guest house. She had long desired to see the world, but Ansige's strong dislike of travel and utter dependence on her had thwarted that dream soon after their marriage.

She made preparations. She began to compile her recipes, printing them carefully in hardcover books and then putting the books into an old biscuit tin where they would be sealed away and protected from damp and vermin. She took up her savings, money earned from her share of the family's lands and livestock. She did this swiftly and quietly, because she did not wish to discuss with her family what she could not fully explain. Part of her still refused to believe in the mysterious stranger, but if there were such a person, all the better that she should leave Makendha to keep her family safe.

Then she began to tell her family by degrees.

'I think I need a small vacation, a change of scenery. You can spare me for a few weeks, can't you Maa?'

And later, more seriously, to her father:

'I can't stay here forever, you know. Our lands were never intended to support so many husbandless daughters. Let me go up to the House of the Sisters and see what work they may have for me.'

Semwe listened to the words and what he thought was behind them, and reluctantly gave his approval. He thought that she was seeking a sense of worth after her failed, childless marriage, desiring a status that could not be found as an adult under her parents' roof.

'But a few weeks only, as you hinted to your mother,' he said, raising a finger in caution. 'Then you must come back, and we will talk again.'

Paama agreed.

She said nothing at all to her sister, which, in retrospect, may have been a mistake.

Taran arrived, ironically, with exactly the entrance Ansige had hoped to have. He rode a fine horse at the head of a small procession of servants and pack animals. On arrival, he sent his majordomo ahead to the chief to present a gift and his compliments, and to convey his formal request to pitch camp in the fields near Makendha. This was a common practice for nomad merchant princes, so the chief happily accepted the generous gift and sent back one of his own servants to guide Taran to Makendha's pastures and woods.

The entire train wound through the streets of Makendha. People stared and muttered, and behind his veil Taran stared back, eyes glittering coldly. He was looking for a familiar face, and listening for a familiar voice.

But nothing has as fine a sense of drama and comedy as chaos. Thus it was that Paama, leading a single mule for a pack animal and carrying the Stick at her belt, left by the back roads which went up towards the hills and completely missed Taran's arrival into Makendha.

10

PAAMA AMONG THE SISTERS,
AND ALTON THE POET FINDS HIS MUSE

MANY TIMES HAS THE TALE been told of the composer Lewis and how, fasting, he spent a full day and a night creating his famous chorus *Entry into the Courts of Heaven*, a chorus which would become the axis, the centrepiece of the latter portion of his symphonic diptych *Redemption*. After completing it, he was moved to tears and declared that it needed no revision, for he had but recorded the music exactly as he had heard it when, transported from his study, he had stood in those very courts with angels thronging to the left and right of him.

Less embraced by oral history is the equally interesting tale of *Jacob's Ladder*, the centrepiece of the first half of *Redemption*, which, though almost as renowned and adored as *Courts of Heaven*, caused him many pangs of labour to deliver live and not stillborn. Inspiration had been in such short supply that he had been constrained to cobble together pieces from his musical ragbag, that collection of orphaned snippets of likely pieces whose greater works had either suffered from drought or block at a critical point, or which, though performanceworthy, had been deemed unfashionable by patrons and were thus abandoned as unprofitable. To the trained ear it was evident—new lyrics sat oddly on musical trills that had been tailored to fit other, more secular words—and yet the public loved it and found in it something near to that other, effortless God gift.

Paama knew of both tales and often consoled herself that since very few people could tell the difference between gross human toil and sublime heavenly message, there might be an element of the heavenly in the former, and of the human in the latter. She had never realised that others thought the same way until she saw the legend on the arch of the gate to the House of the Sisters:

Work is Prayer.

She rang the gate's bell and waited.

A woman shuffled down the dusty path, her head bound in a simple cotton wrap, her feet in mended canvas shoes. She was familiar to Paama, but it was not until she was much closer to the gate that her old eyes brightened in recognition at the sight of her visitor.

'Paama, come in, come in and welcome! How good to see you.' She fumbled back the gate's iron latch and opened the way for Paama and her mule to enter.

'Aunty Jani,' Paama said, embracing her warmly, cheek to aged cheek.

It was the wrong form of address, of course, but Sister Jani had known Paama from her youngest days and had been an aunty for longer than she had been a sister.

'Will you take in a kitchen helper for a few weeks?'

Sister Jani laughed. 'Kitchen helper—you? Please, take over with my blessing. But you did not come all the way up here just to cook for us, did you?'

With that mild encouragement, Paama suddenly found herself pouring out the story of her bizarre life, starting with when Ansige came to Makendha to fetch her back home. She talked for so long that the mule grew bored and started to chew at her sleeve, and still she was only to the point where Ansige tumbled into the well. Sister Jani pulled the mule away, and they laughed together for a moment.

'Let us give this one something more nourishing to chew on and take your bags into the House,' suggested Sister Jani.

Within an hour or so, Paama was sitting on a mat before a low table set with simple but delicious refreshments: fruit, soft cheese, semisweet cakes laden with nuts, and the drink the House had made famous—lime juice with just the right proportions of mint and ginger. She managed to eat and continue her tale. When she reached the part about the djombi, she hesitated and then went on cautiously, speaking in vague terms about having received a gift and a warning. Sister Jani gave her a long, close look that had nothing to do with physical near-sightedness, but she said nothing until Paama came to the end.

'I think that you have come to consult with a Reader,' she said.

Paama kept silent. She had thought nothing of the kind, but suddenly it seemed an excellent idea. The House of the Sisters was renowned for its scholars and wisewomen. The Readers of the House represented one of the special branches of learning of which she knew little, but she had heard of people consulting them for problems that could not be solved by herbwomen or surgeons.

She did not know what to expect and was therefore more than a little startled when Sister Jani led her to a large room where a woman stood at a joiner's worktable assembling what looked like shelving. The woman looked up, wiping her hands free of sawdust on her apron.

'Someone for a Reading, then?' she said cheerfully, seemingly not bothered about being disturbed midtask.

She untied the apron and tossed it on top of the table. Motioning Paama over to sit on a long bench by the wall, she pulled up a stool and positioned herself in front of her.

'This is Paama, Sister Elen,' said Sister Jani. 'Can you help her?'

'We'll see,' smiled Sister Elen. 'Tell me your story.'

Paama began slowly at first, but soon the words flowed. Sister Jani withdrew so quietly that Paama did not even realise when she left, but by then Sister Elen seemed so well known to her that there was no self-consciousness in her. She did not trim the facts this time but told the full story while the patient listener opposite sucked it in as if she were a benign vacuum. Then, at last, it was over, and there was a long silence during which the Reader stared at the silk-wrapped Stick fastened to Paama's belt.

'I think,' she said slowly, 'that you should consult with our Speaker. Follow me.'

Bemused, Paama let the woman lead her through passages and doorways into a cool storeroom where a sister was diligently labelling and listing the sealed containers on the shelves.

'Sister Deian. This is Paama. I have read her story, but there is more to it than meets the eye. Perhaps you could do a Speaking for us?'

Sister Deian turned from her work and greeted Paama. Paama was dismayed to see that in contrast to the warmth and welcome she had so far encountered, Sister Deian's face was not friendly but tense, as if Paama represented something she would rather not face. For the first time, Paama felt tainted, like one with a contagious disease.

'There will be no Speaking for this one, I fear. Her tale is true, and that is all I can say. More than that is impossible with that thing in her keeping.'

She nodded towards the Stick, and her expression was that of someone determined not to show the fear she was feeling.

'She had better go straight to a Dreamer, perhaps,' mused Sister Elen. 'I hope you are willing to spend a little time with us, Paama. Dreaming is not quickly done, and more than one Dream must be examined for a full understanding.'

'Will I be safe here?' Paama asked, suddenly feeling vulnerable and exposed, like a person who wakes to find she has walked in her sleep into the middle of a battlefield.

'Why, Paama! You're worried about *your* safety? With that you could protect all of us,' said Sister Deian.

Paama found that to be even more worrying.

✳

A spare pasture near Makendha had been selected for Lord Taran's temporary address, and it now sprouted a tent city with one large palatial tent at the centre and a few satellites sprinkled about its circumference. One of the smaller tents was occupied by the man whom Taran had hired to speak for him all the words that a djombi would never say and could never mean. He was pretending to set his pens and writing desk and other paraphernalia in order, but in reality he was brooding.

Alton the poet was a man setting out on a long journey for the first time. Because he did not look young, people assumed that he had been a long time at his job and must be something of a master. The reality was that premature greying had crowned him with an appearance of greater maturity than was actually the case. He truly was a poet, but a very young one who was only now testing out ways to make money from his art ... if art it was. A terribly shy man, he was far too self-deprecating, an unhelpful trait in any person who aims to sell snatches of empty air shaped around vowels and consonants, or worse, bits of white paper irregularly stained with black ink.

When he had been hired by Bini, he had mistaken the majordomo for the master, but when he saw who the master really was, his worries increased. Once, he would have thought himself beyond fortunate to be in the household of a rich merchant prince, but fantasies and dreams worked well enough when unfulfilled. Now he would have to produce work worthy of his exalted position, and the muse in him fled in terror at the thought.

On reaching Makendha, he relaxed slightly. This was the kind of village that a city man like himself rarely took seriously. It was his own fault, perhaps, that he was so lulled and vulnerable when Bini called him into his tent-office to receive his first assignment.

'You are to write a love poem.'

Alton looked at him, expecting more, but Bini's face was poker-bland.

'Just . . . a love poem? Might I ask for whom? I mean . . . I don't want to be nosy, but it helps if you can imagine who . . . who you're writing to . . . and maybe why you're writing to them? Or is this just an arbitrary love poem?' he stammered.

'There is a woman named Neila in Makendha. Her mother is Tasi, her father is Semwe, and she is not yet married. The poem is to be addressed to her, and it will be signed by our lord. Then you will deliver it to her, orally as well as on paper.'

Alton flinched. His penmanship had always been excellent, but his oratory was more of a challenge.

'By tomorrow,' Bini concluded.

Deadlines were the one thing guaranteed to pour ice water all over Alton's creativity. He fished for help, something to delay the inevitable.

'I have not even seen the subject. Where will I get my inspiration?'

Bini got up from his desk and patiently led the young man out of the tent. He pointed across the pastures towards the edge of the village, where young women were fetching water from the village well. 'Go and see. Try not to get too inspired.'

Alton set off, trying to appear unconcerned. Women fell into that category of fantasies and dreams that worked well when unfulfilled but presented all kinds of problems when brought out into the real world of trial and failure. Only his greater fear of being fired pushed him on towards the well and took his trembling legs to the edge of the group of chattering women. A few fell silent and gave him that dismissive, up-and-down flash of the eye that women could be so horribly good at. The rest ignored him.

Then one of the women turned around.

It was exactly like the master poets had written it. The air seemed to turn hollow, muting the sound of chatter to mere background warbles. The other women became like so much wallpaper, a neutral backdrop for the vividness of the central figure. He heard a voice say:

'You must be Neila. I am Alton, poet of the household of the Lord Taran.'

This could hardly be his own voice. It rolled, it thundered boldly, it was the voice of one who knew that he would be heard. Giddy with this unlooked-for power, he continued speaking, fuelled by a rare vintage of courage.

This was not Taran's doing. Taran might have done something, perhaps if the first draft of a poem had come for his signature and had proved substandard, but he had not even heard Alton speak as yet. What Alton did was not at all remarkable. Like many men before him, he had simply fallen in love with the face of the most beautiful woman in the village, and in so doing had found his muse.

11

HOW TO WOO A LADY

ALTON'S LOVE POEMS TO NEILA have been famous for years, as everyone knows, but if you want to sample them for yourself, or try a verse or two on your own beloved, I fear that you will have to buy the published works or attend one of the performances still running in theatres in many of the major cities. A minor writer such as I cannot afford the cost of reproducing the words of the poet dubbed Love's Own Laureate.

We don't need to focus on Alton's poetry, anyway. What is far more interesting is the effect it was having on Neila. She had had all kinds of unsophisticated men try to win her affection, or at least her attention, by rough, bumbling shows of their love. She had grown immune to such behaviour. She had also had suave, rich men of the world come with dazzling gifts and earnest charm, but these too had left her cold. Into this vast range of possibility strolled Alton. He had the touching gormlessness of the poor young lads, but he was backed by the wealth and authority of a rich suitor. Moreover, he brought something new and fascinating. When viewed from a certain angle, he was weak, timid, and unprepossessing. Then he looked at her and became visibly transformed into a classical hero. It made her feel incredibly powerful. Many women, by their beauty and sheer presence, have reduced intelligent men to babbling idiots or gaping mutes, but few have inspired to such heights of eloquence a man who can only be described as mediocre.

There is the secret. Show a woman that she has the power to improve you a thousand times over, and she is yours for life.

Unfortunately, Alton was not being paid to woo in his own name, and everyone knew it. Semwe frowned a lot but decided to leave it to Tasi to warn Neila about the tragic triangle that was forming before their eyes. Tasi spoke quietly and briefly, reminding Neila that in paying attention to Alton's addresses, she was in fact encouraging the mysterious, faceless lord.

Neila's own feelings were very complex. Alton made her feel deified, but the veiled stranger who had sent him had another, additional cachet. Once, as he was about to ride past her on one of the outer trails to the pasture, he slowed his horse and slightly inclined his head. She stood still, speechless and staring, as his eyes looked at her and into her as if they would burn through the veil, and burn her up, too. She saw the strange colour—another thing that stunned her—and felt bizarrely shaken when at last he turned away and spurred his horse on.

She wondered why he so shrouded himself, and she even asked Alton if he was wooing her to be the bride of a monster, but Alton, being of the albinism hypothesis party, soon reassured her—incorrectly of course—that her suitor was entirely human, albeit one who looked as if he had been dipped in milk.

There's another secret. Mystery with a touch of fear is a powerful attractor. It is an excellent aid to wooing, however it is extremely difficult, if not impossible, to maintain.

Taran made himself be patient. He realised that he had to give Alton time to prepare the ground before he stepped in, but he was also delaying a formal meeting with Neila and her family for two other reasons. First, he was trying to detect once more that delicate sense of chaos, but for some reason, he could not find anything throughout all the village of Makendha. He found a satisfactory reason—that she must have been warned about his arrival and was now hiding the power—and put that thought aside. Second, he was bracing himself to speak to humans again. Bini gave him some practice, but he was a servant taking orders from his lord. Taran could not speak to Semwe, Tasi, and Neila in the same fashion.

He tried walking about in the woods and practising, using drafts of Alton's poetry as his primer. After a week, he decided he was ready. He would have a banquet and invite the chief, some other Makendha notables, and Neila and her family.

When Alton learned of this, he became instantly depressed. He bore the invitation, written in his own hand and sealed by his lord, to Neila. It depressed him further when he saw how her eyes widened in excitement at the thought of meeting Lord Taran in his own domicile.

'Shall I tell my lord that you are pleased to accept his invitation?' he asked coldly.

She could not miss his distant tone. 'Alton, won't I see you there?'

'Not as a guest, but as a servant,' he replied gloomily. 'My lady, I have bewitched myself into believing that I was on my own errand, and not that of another man. I have injured my own heart. You are not to blame.'

'You can write a poem about it,' his muse said shrewdly, if callously, and, leaving him there muttering new verses under his breath, she dashed off to tell her parents.

Tasi insisted that Neila have a new dress for the occasion, but there was hardly enough time to send to Ahani for a truly fashionable new outfit, so she took some of her savings and went to bribe a neighbour to give up some of the silk she had been saving for her own daughter's wedding. It was a beautiful piece of fabric, pale gold embroidered with ivory thread, and it needed only a simple cut to flatter Neila's skin and figure.

Semwe, too, was dipping into his savings and anxiously consulting with the chief on what would be a suitable gift for his daughter's rich, foreign suitor. He heard the chief's advice with some relief—not only was the suggestion within his means, but he knew exactly where a very fine example of such workmanship could be found. He sent out a message in haste, praying that there would be enough time for the work to be done.

A small boy rode up the back roads to the hills on a mule. He was a regular visitor; he carried letters, packages, and other sundries up to the House of the Sisters and took similar cargo back down the hill to Makendha. He reached the gate, slid off the mule's back, and rattled the bell loudly.

Paama came running to the gate. 'Hush, child, we're not all hard of hearing. What do you have for us today?'

'Mornin', Aunty Paama. Letters, and a parcel for Sister Elen.'

He dug envelopes out of a canvas bag and gave them to her and then untied the cords that fastened the parcel to the back of his rough saddle. Paama took them all and piled them up neatly. As she did so, one of the envelopes made her pause.

'Thank you,' she said to the postboy absently, and started to walk briskly back inside.

Sister Elen was passing near the door as she entered. Paama gave her the parcel, blindly, eyes still fixed on the envelope.

'Here, this is for you.'

She put the other letters in their accustomed place on the table by the door and held out the envelope that had so held her attention. 'And this, it seems, is for you and for me.'

Sister Elen looked mildly surprised. She took the envelope, opened it, and read the contents quickly.

'An order for the House. Your father wants us to make a travelling stool with all the traditional carvings suitable for a minor chief. He hasn't given us much time! And for you, an invitation. Your sister is being courted by a foreign merchant prince, and he is having a dinner in your sister's honour.'

Paama's eyes widened. 'In two weeks all this can happen? Maa must be very proud of Neila.'

Sister Elen did not seem quite as excited. She was frowning as if something very worrying had occurred to her.

'What is it, Sister?' Paama asked her.

'I am thinking of something that Sister Carmis said.'

Sister Carmis was a Dreamer. She, too, had listened to Paama's story, and then she had gone away without saying a word to anyone. No-one had told Paama what was supposed to happen after that, except that she had to be patient.

'What did she say, and why didn't she tell me?' Paama complained.

'Dreaming is very imprecise. It is not always possible to separate the true dreams from the ramblings of the sleeping mind. We prefer to wait until there is a clear sign that a dream is significant. Be patient a little longer, Paama. I must consult with my sisters.'

Paama was left to wonder and fret and speculate for the rest of the day. When news finally came, it was Sister Jani who brought it to her.

'Paama, you must go back to Makendha and protect your sister,' she said bluntly.

Paama looked at the expression of bleak worry on the face before her and said softly, 'Is that all you have to tell me?'

'Sister Carmis has had a dream that is very difficult to read. There will be strife between you and a stranger, but she cannot tell what will happen in the end. Your sister must not stand between the two of you, or there could be grave trouble for her.'

'I'll go now,' Paama said, her face grim and her eyes anxious.

'No. Wait a while. We must do all that we can to prepare you.'

'Can you teach me to use the Stick any better than the djombi did?' Paama asked with some bitterness.

Sister Jani laughed without humour. 'No. But we can give you such assistance as our own talents provide.'

Paama could not guess what she meant by this, but when she began to pack her belongings, the four sisters came to her, all bearing packages.

Sister Elen stepped forward first and gave her a tiny box, small enough to fit into her hand. 'This is a brooch, but it will also allow me to Read the stranger. Be sure to wear it on your dress when you go to the dinner.'

Then it was the turn of Sister Deian. The package she gave to Paama was slightly larger than her hand. 'This is a hairband. When you wear it, you will hear my voice behind your ear Speaking the truth about the stranger.'

Sister Carmis, the quietest of the sisters whom Paama had encountered, came forward with a large, light parcel. 'Place this cushion under your head at night, and I will be with you in your dreams, to show you what may be, and to guard you against what must not be.'

Paama stared at the sisters and at her gifts, overwhelmed. 'Thank you. I feel less afraid now.'

'But not less careful,' warned Sister Jani.

Paama looked at the last package, which was so large that Sister Jani had rested it on the floor the moment she entered the room.

'And what is that?' she said in trepidation.

'The carved stool for your father's gift. Do be careful taking it down the hill. Sister Elen was forced to rush the gluing, and too much movement will shake the joints loose again.'

12

THE FACE BEHIND THE VEIL

PAAMA'S RETURN TO MAKENDHA WAS as quiet and fuss-free as her departure had been. Although her family was expecting her, their welcome was a touch harried, and her father was actually slightly more cheerful about seeing the stool completed than about seeing his daughter again.

Neila was glad to see her, an unusual state of affairs. She was happy to have someone to talk to about Alton and the man who had sent him, the man who hid his face. Paama listened with more attention than she was accustomed to giving to her years-younger sister and her busy love life. There was more than one stranger in Makendha, and she needed to find out which was the one to beware of.

'Let me see if I have it straight,' she said, gently pausing her sister in midflow. 'Alton is a poet, and he speaks beautiful words to you, and you are very interested in him . . . is that right?'

Neila nodded, beaming radiantly.

'Then there is Lord Taran, whose face no-one has seen, but who is tall, silent, has eyes like amethyst—so far as you have been able to observe, that is—and is very rich. And you are also very interested in him.'

Neila shamelessly nodded again.

'Which one are you considering for marriage again? I have forgotten.'

Neila gave her a hurt look. 'Lord Taran, as you well know. Alton is only his servant.'

'Hmm,' Paama said doubtfully. 'And are there any other men of note in this Lord Taran's household?'

Neila stared at her. 'I thought you were tired of men and marriage.'

Paama gave her an equally blank stare in reply before she understood the meaning of her sister's words. 'Not for me, silly child. I . . . I just want to know.'

Neila smiled in disbelief. 'There are only a few minor servants . . . and the one who heads the household, of course, but he is not very interesting.'

Paama was not reassured. She had seen a djombi make do with the shadow of a six year-old girl and still achieve its purpose. Her enemy might be the mysterious lord, or the extraordinarily gifted poet, but he could just as easily be the boring majordomo, or one of the minor servants—perhaps even the one who would bear the cup of welcome when she first entered the tent of the merchant prince. She would have to meet them all herself and pray that the Sisters' gifts and skills would give her some insight.

On the day of the dinner, Paama made her preparations carefully. She selected a dress that would help her to fade into the background, and she fastened to her belt a matching cloth purse, taking care to arrange it so that the Stick was completely covered. Then she pinned the brooch at the corner of the square neckline and bound her hair back with the headband. The cushion was already waiting by her pillow; she prayed she would need it for nothing more than an ordinary, restful sleep.

At twilight, everyone was ready. Semwe led the way to the tent of Lord Taran, carrying his gift carefully in front of him so as not to wrinkle or stain his best linen tunic. His wife and daughters walked behind him, treading gently in their embroidered cloth slippers, careful to keep to the paving-stone trail. As they approached the tent, they saw that a red carpet had been rolled out from the entrance to the edge of the trail. Neila exclaimed in delight at being treated so royally, but to Paama it resembled a great red tongue waiting to furl up and fling them into the warm glowing maw of the tent's main entrance.

As soon as they stepped off the trail and onto the carpet, a servant came hastening towards them and escorted them in. Paama discreetly turned the brooch in his direction as he guided them to the entrance, but nothing happened, no lightning flash, no sound of alarm. Then she entered and forgot about him instantly. The lanterns hanging from the ceiling were shaded with amber-tinted glass, heating the cool evening air to an uncomfortable temperature and making the very air ruddy. However, when Paama looked around at the guests in the reception area, everyone appeared contented and relaxed, sipping iced drinks and marvelling at the sumptuous interior of the merchant's tent. Many of the faces were known to her, but she remembered Giana and shuddered. It could be anyone.

She tried to copy them, tried not to look suspicious of everything and everybody, but even the servant who offered her a drink from a tray seemed to be secretly laughing at her. That was a horrible thought. She was looking for one adversary, but suppose they were all part of it, willing co-conspirators for their own gain? She drank gingerly, alert to any alien flavour, and sighed. Paranoia was an exhausting state to be in.

Neila nudged her. 'There's Alton.'

She pointed out a man with an expression of discomfort on his face, a young face under greying hair. He looked slightly out of place, the usual appearance for those whose status was neither guest nor visibly busy servant. Paama wondered if he would perform one of his works later in the evening, or if he was there to soak up more inspiration for another poem. She touched the Stick idly through her bag, hoping vaguely that it could help her in some way, but it was as ordinary as any piece of wood.

'Paama.'

The ghostly voice made her jump, and she stared at the Stick before she remembered the purpose of the headband she wore.

'Paama, Sister Elen says that the young man before you is not all that he seems. He has the mark of alteration upon him. Be careful of him.'

So, it *was* him! And he looked so harmless, so timid and self-effacing. She pulled her horrified gaze away before he noticed her stare.

'And that one,' continued Neila, 'is the head man.'

Paama looked in the opposite direction and saw a man standing on the other side of the room. He had quite a different air. Although he, too, seemed to have nothing to do, he did it splendidly, his eye on every servant, every tray, measuring the speed of service and the quantity of food and drink, and issuing orders with the smallest of nods. Only once did he need to beckon someone over and whisper, perhaps to make a more forceful point that could not be conveyed by a gesture. His eyes were ... flat, expressionless. He could have been a piece of furniture animated for the evening.

'This one also bears the mark of alteration. Watch him closely.'

Paama was shocked. How was this possible? Could he be manipulating two at the same time? Sister Deian anticipated her question.

'It may be that they have had their memories altered, nothing more,' she cautioned. 'These are probably the men who have spoken to him directly.'

'And that's Lord Taran,' breathed Neila.

A tall man, veiled and robed in ivory linen, came up and greeted Semwe, courteously thanking him for his gift. He ignored the three women, but Paama knew that was only more courtesy according to his

culture. He would pretend that they did not exist until Semwe intro-
duced them, thus giving him permission to speak to them.

'My wife, Tasi,' Semwe said.

The foreign prince bowed, his hands clasped decorously behind
his back. Paama noticed that he was also gloved, and she began to
understand somewhat Neila's fascination with this man who exposed
not even a finger's breadth of his skin to the air.

'My daughters, Paama and Neila.'

Neila lowered her eyes modestly, but Paama boldly searched the
small, blurred rectangle of mesh for a glimpse of his eyes. Was he the
one? Was he surprised to see her? Did he know who she was at all?

'Ladies,' he said, and there was nothing but warm welcome in his
tone. 'I am honoured to have you in my humble home.'

'Is it really your home, my lord?' Paama said, speaking her thought
out loud and shocking herself with her boldness. 'I mean, since you
are travelling this is surely nothing more than a temporary abode.'

The blank face of cloth turned towards her. 'I am a nomad, my
lady. Wherever we sleep for more than three days, we call it home.'

Neila nudged her for her impudence, but she did not care. What
she did care about was the fact that she had as yet heard nothing from
the Sisters on how Lord Taran appeared to them. He spoke for a while
longer with them, trivial pleasantries about the virtues of Makendha
and its countryside, and then excused himself to speak to other guests.

'—probably the centre of it.' Sister Deian's voice cut in suddenly,
and then stopped.

'What?' Paama said, speaking aloud in her frustration and earning
another nudge from Neila.

She had forgotten that the Sisters could not hear her. Something
had stopped Sister Deian's voice from reaching her, something that
was 'probably the centre'. That was no puzzle—the mystery man must
be the enemy after all. She had a strong desire to tear that veil away.

Dinner held no drama. The food was good, but to the trained palate of a chef, it was not approaching excellence. Lord Taran was the main attraction, showing himself to be as civilised a barbarian as ever pitched a tent on the pastures of Makendha. He spoke intelligently and listened attentively and was in every way the kind of gentleman that mothers would wish to have their daughters marry. His expressive voice compensated grandly for the formless sheet before his face. Paama saw her parents glance at each other and give a little nod. His charm was magical, winning the hearts of all his guests—all except Paama.

After dinner, they all went outside for the entertainment, which consisted of a grand show of firestars. It was a well-chosen diversion; the whole village could see it and enjoy it, and the next day there would be a rush to order firestars from the merchant's stores. As the guests sat under the true stars and watched the spectacle, Lord Taran's servants ranged the fields with buckets of water and wet rags, carefully slapping out the few stray sparks that still glowed after the spent firestars had fallen to earth.

'Where is your sister?' came Sister Deian's voice, sudden and frantic.

Paama jumped up as if she had been singed by a firestar and looked around wildly. Neila's chair was empty! She excused herself hastily, but her departure went unnoticed as all were captivated by a sky full of glittering meteors and coloured fire. Wishing again for some help from the Stick, she touched it almost superstitiously as she set off in a random direction, hoping that would be where she would find her sister. Sure enough, there was the sound of her voice . . .

'Let me go!'

Paama began to run, but just then a hand gripped her arm firmly above the elbow.

'Where are you going? It's dangerous to go roaming about in the dark.'

She wrenched around, but her arm was still held fast in a strong hand.

'You!' she hissed.

Lord Taran put a hand over her mouth. 'Hush! Not so loud.'

One hand remained free. She grabbed a fistful of veil and pulled as hard as she could... and stared. He let her go and stepped away, looking at her in dismay.

'You!' she said again, her heart pounding more in confusion than fear. 'Then where is... who is...'

She ran again, towards where she had last heard her sister's voice. There she saw two figures struggling in the dark. One was the poet, Alton, his young face aged with fury as he shook Neila by the shoulders.

'Give it back to me, you thief! You don't understand such power, you'll only misuse it!'

Neila screamed and broke away from him, then ran to Paama and fell sobbing into her arms. Paama held her securely for a brief moment of comfort and then shook her by the shoulders and forced her chin up.

'Neila, look at them. *Look* at them!'

The man who had been veiled walked cautiously towards the sisters and then around them, and stood next to the poet. Two men were before them, the lord and the poet, both standing very still as if trying to think of what to do next. Neila looked from one face to the other, her tears silenced in her shock. Then she cried out in anguished query to the man who had worn the veil.

'Alton?'

The lord stood with hands limp at his sides like a puppet with cut strings, looking at her with an expression of pure bewilderment. Paama could not understand why, for was it not Neila who had the right to bewilderment, faced with two copies of the same man? One was dressed as suitor and the other as servant, but both had the face of the poet Alton.

The man dressed as the poet sighed, a harsh sigh of frustration and annoyance. 'I don't have time to play this farce any more. Let us talk plainly.'

He stretched out his hand with a grasping motion, and stillness seized the night like spreading ice quelling a river current. The popping sounds of the firestars, the screech of the crickets, and the chirp of the tree frogs were all halted in the space of one slow heartbeat. Then he stepped closer to Paama and Neila, his figure blurring, his features changing, his skin becoming a deep indigo under the white glow of a firestar frozen above. Paama, too, was frozen—frozen with deep fear.

'Now I have all the time in the world,' he said in a chill voice that little resembled the warm tones he had borrowed from the poet. 'Give me my power back, and I will allow you to forget that this ever happened.'

13

ONE STAR RISES, ANOTHER STAR SETS

DO NOT THINK BADLY OF Paama. She had never had any experience of being a heroine, and she was not accustomed to otherworldly beings threatening her loved ones. So it was courage of a sort that made her step in front of Neila, whip out the Stick . . . and offer it to the indigo lord.

His eyes narrowed in suspicion, but he took another step closer and stretched out his hand. Neila ran from Paama with another shriek of fear and went straight to the arms of Alton, who was not so dazed that he did not react appropriately, holding her protectively and shielding her face from the awful scene playing out before her. Paama had no refuge; she stood her ground and trembled as that unearthly blue hand closed slowly over the Stick.

The Stick would not move. He tugged it fiercely, she opened her palms wide, but it stuck to her like an extension of her own hand. He stopped pulling and became strangely calm, almost analytical, as he held her wrists gently and turned his head to view the phenomenon from all angles.

'Perhaps if I cut her hands off?' he mused to himself.

Neila gave a low moan and Paama's breath choked off in the middle of her suddenly constricted throat.

Just when it seemed impossible to be any more shocked and

terrified, a new thing happened. A bizarrely shaped figure loomed out of the stilled outside world and casually tore open their little bubble of time, holding the edges apart carefully with sharp-tipped, multiple, hairy legs.

'They're coming,' it said.

It was half Bini, half the trickster spider. The dead human eyes remained as blank as any mere decoration, but the spider eyes glittered avidly with pure mischief. The indigo lord did not quite show surprise, but his eyes narrowed again and his lips pressed together angrily as if he were thinking, *I might have known.*

'You'd better clear up this mess before you go,' the spider continued with infuriating superiority.

The indigo lord looked as if he would have liked to snarl at the Trickster, but from the sudden shadow in his eyes, it was clear that another sense was warning him of the truth of the Trickster's words. He closed his eyes for a moment and looked at Neila and Alton, and then he glared at the Trickster.

'You helped start it; you can finish it off,' he said, punctuating his curt words with an impatient gesture.

The bubble shrank, pulling swiftly away from the Trickster's snatching pincers, drawing smoothly past and through the tightly intertwined forms of Neila and Alton, and centring at last on Paama and the indigo lord. Far too late, she made a movement to dash away, but he looked at her with an expression of deep satisfaction and gently folded the bubble in with one last, lazy curl of his fingers.

It was as if some small piece of the world had silently imploded and extruded itself elsewhere, and the unseen breach had pinched off and healed itself over like a cell budding off from its parent. When it was done, the Trickster, Alton, and Neila stood staring at the empty space that had held Paama and the indigo lord. The Trickster sighed gently. He would have enjoyed the chase, but the indigo lord had been right. He was bound to help tidy up the loose ends.

Once more ordinary in his form of Bini the majordomo, he looked at Alton's memory, then at Neila's, and grinned at the excellent adjustment that the indigo lord had achieved in the brief seconds before his departure. It would truly be a pleasure to build on this tale.

'My lord, it appears that your disguise has been discovered.'

Alton frowned as if trying to recall something, and then nodded slowly as Neila gazed up at him.

'Are you disappointed in me, love? It was the only way I could get to know you without all this getting in the way.' He swept his hand to indicate the gorgeous tent, the brilliant firestars, and his own princely attire.

Neila's eyes were adoring. 'All the qualities I love are together in one man. How could I be disappointed?'

The Trickster smiled and withdrew . . . but I am hearing some rumblings from my audience. You are distressed that I have spoiled the moving and romantic tale of how Love's Laureate courted his beautiful wife? You complain that I have turned it into a cobbled pastiche of happenstance, expediency, and the capricious tricks of the djombi? I bleed for your injured sentiments, but to dress the tale in vestments of saga and chivalry was never my intent. A sober and careful reading of history will teach you that both lesser and greater persons have been treated more roughly by fate. Be content. If it was only a djombi's vanity and aversion to human company that caused Alton to become a merchant prince for one night, if it was fear of discovery and capture that made that djombi flee, thus settling a lordly mantle on Alton for all time, how does that come to be my fault? I am only the one who tells the story.

So, while the young lovers kiss under a firestar-filled sky, while the Trickster glides among the guests—ever the discreet servant—and quietly adjusts memories that might contradict what is to become the official version of events, while all these reasonably amazing things are happening, there is something more out there in the night. A ripple, perhaps, in reality; an extra shiver that tingles along the spine that can be attributed to the firestars, or to kisses. Certainly there is nothing else to be seen.

The djombi are coming.

Bini straightens and stiffens as he feels the equivalent of someone tugging at his sleeve.

A voice inaudible to humans rings in his ear. 'Where are they?'

He shrugs it off, murmurs softly, 'I may be a trickster, but even I know better than to interfere in affairs of this kind.'

'You interfered quite beautifully when you told him about Paama. Why stop now?'

'I have my orders. Sometimes I even carry them out. I can't stay a trickster forever, you know.'

The djombi swirl away, disappointed, and continue their hunt for their apostate comrade.

I am the last person in the world who should be speculating on the motives of the djombi and the reasons they have for acting as they do, but I cannot help contrasting the Trickster with the indigo lord. I have a suspicion that the Trickster began as tricksters do, delighting in the frailties of humans and exploiting those weaknesses for his own entertainment. The junior tricksters who led Ansige on his merry dance to ruin would have been impressed by some of his earlier exploits, and indeed many of these had become legend. However, of late he had become almost staid and boring. If I were to hazard a guess, I would say that he had unwittingly become fond of the creatures he was so accustomed to torturing, and tired of playing the same old practical jokes. He had gradually changed his modus operandi, taking up the greater challenge of turning people to situations of mutual benefit rather than merely gratifying his own sense of the ridiculous.

The indigo lord had come from the other direction. Assigned to the protection and improvement of humankind, he found himself dismayed and disillusioned by humans and their flaws. It was like being made to play with broken toys, and the moment a few were fixed to some degree of functionality, a fresh set of broken ones was pushed his way. First he grew proud, then contemptuous, and finally uncaring. His sense of honour would not permit him to do as the tricksters do, and either way he prided himself that his sense of humour was too sophisticated for him to be amused by the pratfalls and pie-faces of a pitifully lesser breed. Having lost common purpose with his colleagues, and unable to find common ground with his adversaries, he was content to isolate himself . . . and would have continued to do only that if it had not been for the partial stripping of his powers.

I think that by strange chance the Trickster had risen even as the indigo lord had fallen. The Trickster was now tentatively taking on the 'orders' that the indigo lord was refusing to carry out. And yet even the Trickster had his version of pride . . . to admit that he was pushing his toe past the line was something that he was not yet prepared to do. So, trust him not, but do not believe that all his actions are intended for the ruin of those affected, human or djombi. I, too, shall have to wait until the tale is fully told before I can be sure which way he will turn.

One of the consequences of that night was that Paama's disappearance was not immediately noticed, because one of the memories that Bini chose to blur was Paama's attendance at the dinner. However, the heart of Semwe warned him that something did not feel right about what his mind was telling him. Baffled and concerned, he wrote a letter to the House of the Sisters.

Dear Sister Jani,
    Please thank Sister Elen for her swift and excellent craftsmanship. I believe she will soon see more orders for similar furniture coming from our resident merchant prince.

Have you any word for me from Paama? I thought she was coming to the dinner, but perhaps she slipped away. I was a bit preoccupied at the time, so I may have missed what she was telling me about her future plans.

All the best to those in the House.

Semwe

A reply came back to Semwe with unusual swiftness, as if it had been penned and sent immediately with the postboy.

Dear Semwe

Do not worry about your elder daughter. Paama is away on an errand for us. We promise to look after her for you.

She may have left a cushion on her bed when she left. Please keep it safe for her. You and Tasi may find it a comfort to use it from time to time.

Congratulations on the engagement of your younger daughter. We understand that the gentleman in question is a talented poet and a wealthy businessman. You are very fortunate to be gaining a son-in-law of that calibre. There are so many tricksters about in this world.

Blessings from your friends at the House.

Jani, Elen, Deian and Carmis

Semwe found that this letter took away very little of his bafflement and concern, but he was at least reassured by their promise to look after Paama. It was the comment about his prospective son-in-law that made him uneasy. What he would do to avoid another son-in-law like Ansige!

14

A LESSON IN THE APPROPRIATE USE OF POWER

PAAMA STUMBLED FORWARD AND WAS instantly aware of icy cold hammering up through the soles of her thin slippers like bolts of frozen iron. She was standing on snow. She breathed in, and it felt like a thousand tiny spikes of ice in her nose, throat, and lungs. A cloud blew out of her nostrils as she exhaled. Her eyes prickled and watered in the cold, dry breeze. Everywhere was white.

The indigo lord studied her, his eyes bleakly distant. He walked a few paces away and sat on a snow-covered boulder, apparently immune to the cold, and continued to watch her.

'Put the Stick down by my feet,' he commanded her.

Her half-frozen fingers were clenched tightly around the Stick, but Paama managed to ease her grip, step forward, and stiffly put the Stick down in the thin carpet of snow. He looked at her suspiciously as she edged away and then bent and picked it up.

Nothing happened.

He glared at it and then glared at her. 'You are still holding it.'

'Well, I don't know how I could be, when I'm standing over here!' she snapped at him, frustration overcoming fear. 'And barely standing, at that, as my feet have gone numb. If you are going to kill me, do it now before the cold does it for you!'

He ignored her and turned the inert Stick over in his hands.

Without warning, he raised it in both hands and brought it down hard over his leg. It did not break, though it seemed he could not feel pain. The bafflement and annoyance in his expression increased.

Paama began to shiver violently. 'P-please,' she begged, 'let us get off this mountain—'

'We are not on a mountain,' he corrected absently, still frowning at the Stick. 'We have merely gone south ... very far south.'

'You are killing me,' she whispered.

His answer was to throw the Stick back to her. She caught it clumsily with hands that felt like dead weights on the end of amputated stumps.

'Give it to me again,' he ordered.

Almost vibrating with cold, she obeyed. This time, as he closed his hand over the Stick just above her gripping hand, a sudden squall of sleet drove between them and whipped up the scant covering of snow. The sun, which had been disappearing at intervals behind fast-scudding clouds, blazed out with a brightness magnified several times over by the reflecting snow, and the air sparkled with tiny rainbows.

Paama screamed, and he flung her away from him. As she fell into the wet snow, still holding the Stick, the sleet and wind vanished, the unnatural brightness of the sun diminished, and the rainbows and sparkles disappeared.

'What is that?' he said very seriously, reaching out to touch the Stick again.

Immediately the squall returned in full force and the sun beat fiercely through the swirling whiteness. Paama cowered on the ground, overwhelmed, and waited to die. Then something unexpected and immensely comforting happened.

'Paama!'

It was Sister Deian's voice. Somehow, even at this distance, even after all the drama of recent events, the Sisters were still watching and aware. There was still hope that she could be found. The thought made her raise her head and boldly face her enemy.

'Stop! We cannot hold it together! You will kill us both!' she screamed at him.

He pulled his hand away, bringing the weird weather to an abrupt end, and stared at her. From the look on his face, Paama guessed that he had never been at a loss before.

'I don't want to kill you. I simply want my power back. My power, my own, that which I was made to wield.'

'Then prove it to me,' she panted. 'Let us leave this terrible place before I freeze to death.'

He glanced down at her feet in their thin slippers, now soaked-through with melted snow, and finally understood. With that gesture that was now becoming familiar, he cast out his bubble of time and folded it in until they were somewhere else.

It was like being thrown into an oven. Paama crouched in agony, clasping her hands and pressing her feet as the blood returned painfully to her extremities. Squinting up into the brightness of a noonday sun, she saw the branches of a date palm and felt grass beneath her. Sand dunes curved artistically along the eastern horizon with the austere beauty of deadliness, and the bones of some ruined town stood brokenly on the western horizon.

'Wait here,' the lord said abruptly.

'No!' she shouted. 'Don't leave me here!'

He said impatiently, 'I have told you I am not going to kill you. I am going to get shoes and clothes for you, that is all.'

'Then let me come, too,' she insisted, panicked at the thought of being abandoned.

He shrugged in annoyance and turned away. She got up slowly, teetering on swollen feet, and stumbled after him over the hot, hard-packed sand and gravel.

'Where is this place?' she asked, not expecting to be answered.

'A desert east of the country you know,' he replied vaguely. 'There is treasure . . .' he paused and thumped a foot down on the hard sand '. . . down here.'

He reached out and took her hand without warning, and they fell through the solid ground as if they had suddenly become ghosts. Paama tried to scream but found herself unable to breathe until, with a slight splash, they landed in darkness, ankle deep in gently running water. It was mildly cold and soothing to her burned feet, and the air was moist and cool on her sun-scorched face, but she could not see. He dropped her hand, and she snatched desperately at the air to find where he was standing.

'I cannot see!' she wailed.

'Stop it,' he said, sounding more tired than annoyed.

There was a sizzling noise, and then a flash curved up into the air and froze in a banner of slowly blossoming sparks. He had taken a firestar and thrown it up into the vaulted roof of the vast underground cavern, and now it hung there, somewhat dimmer than usual, but still giving plenty of light for Paama to see around her. Ages of water had carved out this place, and the trickle that now wet her feet was the last remnant of the ancient torrent. The desert above would soon take even that as the sand dunes on the horizon marched on and covered the date palms and the grass.

Then, as she looked a little more closely, she saw evidence of human presence high on the banks of the underground waterway. There were edges in the ground that suggested half-buried crates or boxes, an unnatural colour sticking out of the earth that at a closer glance proved to be cloth dyed purple. She stepped up and out of the water, and there, plainly, were human bones, the long bones of a leg still dressed in the fragments of a half-decayed leather garment, the remainder of the skeleton scattered, as if carried along by random surges of water at the seasonal flood peak.

A clinking noise distracted her from the bones. There was the djombi, very pragmatically filling a sack with gold coins extracted from one of the boxes. Its lock remained intact, but it had been driven against a rock and was split open so that its contents spilled out into the mud.

'What is this place? Who were these people?' she asked.

He stiffened, and then continued to gather up coins as he answered. 'Thieves. Mercenaries. Murderers. They raided and destroyed that place whose ruins you saw above.'

'Why?'

He tied off the sack and said coolly, 'Wars are expensive. Their master had sent them out to get their own wages. The town was not his, and he did not care what happened to it.'

'Then what happened to *them*?'

He looked around the cavern. With his superior sight, the view must have been more terrible; all the bones below the mud were visible to him, and he could glance back in time to see how they had settled there, where they had swept in from, how they had been crushed by rocks and tumbled by water while still in living bodies screaming for help and for mercy.

'I might have got a little carried away,' he murmured.

He seemed to feel Paama's horrified stare, for he turned to her and looked at her sternly. 'I was assigned a very heavy duty. A request had been made that the wealth of this town would never be put to any use that would destroy human life. There was a chance of a thousand-year flood—well, such a flood will not be seen again in this region for tens of thousands of years—and the raiders happened to be in the wrong place at the wrong time when the waters broke through an ancient dam. Chance again brought them and their spoil underground so that now their final tomb is within sight of the town they plundered and desecrated.

Paama transferred her shocked gaze to the Stick. 'Is that the sort of thing this can do?'

'Yes. Hardly the kind of power to be placed in human hands, is it?'

She looked at his alien eyes and the expression of mild contempt in them which had become as constant as a habit, and she felt the need to defend humanity.

'*I* used it to save a boy from drowning. *You* used it to drown an army of men.'

As a jibe, it failed to have any effect. He walked towards her with the sack of gold in one hand and took hold of her wrist with the other. His gaze was not contemptuous but compassionate, as if he did not expect her to be capable of understanding, and recognised that this was not her fault.

'I am sure that they all, boy and army, got exactly what they deserved,' he said.

The firestar woke up from its slow-motion death and gave one last, brilliant splutter before going out for good. Paama felt herself rising, light as air, until the ground was once more under her feet and the blinding sunlight in her face. Before she had a chance to blink twice at the searing brightness, he had released her wrist and was once more making that gathering motion of his hand that warned of another jump to another place.

'I know now what I need to do to you to make you return my power to me,' he remarked almost casually.

And then they were gone again before Paama had time to begin to feel frightened at his words.

15

A LESSON ON CHANCES AND CHOICES

ON THE NIGHT OF THE firestars, all at first was bliss. Alton felt certain that he was indeed a merchant prince, for never before had he taken so much from life's table. The comfort of riches, the sweetness of love, and the beauty of his poetry ravelling out, word by perfect word—it all pointed to a divine will that had blessed him completely. He went to sleep late, crafting couplets to the memory of Neila's kisses.

He awoke the next day in terror and confusion.

'It is only I, my lord.'

Bini approached the bed, breakfast tray held level as he glided smoothly over the thick carpets.

Alton sat up and stared at the vaulted canvas ceiling and the damasked and gilded hangings about his mattress. Had he always bedded down in such luxury? His memory struggled with the vague image of a meagre, dew-damp bedroll flung over small rocks and spiky, tufted grass. Then he raised his puzzled eyes to Bini's calm gaze, and the bothersome vision disappeared.

'Last night was truly a success, my lord. Already we have had several orders for firestars, tapestries, and carpets,' Bini said, his voice as unemotional as ever.

Unable to find a response, Alton watched him set the tray on a low table and pour the breakfast chocolate. The hot liquid spluttered out of the narrow spout of the pot, releasing a welcome fragrance of sweet, cinnamon-rich cocoa. Alton reached out a hand to probe a napkin-lined basket and found warm rolls and pastries tucked inside. He broke off a morsel and ate. Bini finished pouring and stepped back very slightly, hovering with the air of someone anticipating a command. Alton looked at him worriedly.

'Bini,' he asked. 'Have I been ill?'

'Why do you ask, my lord?'

Alton rubbed his head experimentally. It didn't hurt. 'I didn't drink too much last night, did I?'

'I don't know what you mean, my lord.'

'I mean,' said Alton slowly, 'that this all seems...unreal. I know I'm a poet. I've never had a talent for business. Why am I surrounded by prosperity?'

Bini's level gaze did seem to flicker at that point. 'Has my lord forgotten the legacy inherited from his illustrious godfather?'

'N-o,' Alton replied uncertainly.

'The excitement of the engagement has been too much for you. A little more rest...' Bini suggested soothingly.

'Engagement! That memory is true and firm at least!' He threw back the covers energetically, his face illuminated with joy, and came to his feet with a spring.

'My lord, do you have orders for me?' Bini asked gently.

'Orders?'

'For the day's work, the week's operations, the month's pre-planning. Orders.'

Alton's spine lost some of its steely temper. 'I...what do I usually...'

'You usually have breakfast, freshen up, and dress, and then I tell you what new things require attention,' Bini said kindly. There was a hint of a twinkle about his expression, which was very odd considering that his eyes appeared as dead as ever.

That was how Bini began to ease Alton into his new life. He lacked the puppeteer's power of his indigo counterpart, but he had something equally effective—that trickster knack, which was now turned to the benign task of fooling Alton into believing in himself. He mused at the irony; if he did his job well, Alton would never know how much he owed to chance. Illustrious godfather, indeed!

Paama was utterly confused.

They had landed on a hillside overlooking a town unknown to Paama, yet familiar enough in design and outlay that she felt she must be back in her own country, albeit in a province hours ahead of her own Makendha. Rather than murder or torture, the indigo lord's first action towards her was to hand over to her the entire sack of gold and order her to go down to the nearest town and buy for herself more suitable clothes, food, and other necessities.

She placed the coins into her bag beside the Stick, expecting that pickpockets might not find it so easily there, and set off down the road, leaving the djombi standing alone on the hill. Once in town, she found the hour too early for the shops to be open, but not too early for her to gain entry to a guest house. The bandit gold bought a spacious set of rooms with a balcony, a light meal of fruit, and, best of all, no questions. She bathed, ate, and finally, exhausted by travelling half the world in minutes, fell asleep. Remember, she had not slept since the night before.

She did not sleep well or long, for she did not know how long a time she would have before the djombi appeared again. As soon as she saw the first shutters opening, she flew down to the shops. First she bought strong sandals suitable for walking long distances, and then, remembering the snow, she also bought a pair of boots. Both sets of footwear looked ridiculous with her dress, so her next purchases were clothes for travelling, different suits for different climates. By then she was so tired that she returned to her room and fell asleep again.

Her dreams were troubled, filled with the anxieties of her recent experiences. She dreamed she was walking home to Makendha from a far country, and every time she came within sight of her house, the djombi appeared and whisked her back to the other side of the world with a flick of his fingers, forcing her to start the weary trek again and again. After the tenth repetition of this scene, she gave up in disgust and opened her eyes, feeling less rested than when she had first laid down her head.

She was sure she was still dreaming. There was the blue-skinned djombi on the other side of the room, sifting through her purchases with interest. To see an odd and inhuman being doing such an ordinary thing was so incongruous that she forgot to be afraid of him.

'So many things needed,' he commented, knowing that she was awake without looking at her. 'The sun scorches you, the rain drenches you, the rocks tear at your feet, and the wind scours your face. Who would be human?'

He gently threw aside a handful of clothing and sat on the edge of the bed. 'I have figured it out. I cannot take the power of chaos from you, because in your secret heart you believe it is better entrusted to your hands than mine. I cannot blame you. I came to you in disguise, I tried to take it from you by violence, and you judged me by those deeds. I was wrong. I did foolish things because I feared the interference of those who unjustly stole my power. So, let us begin again.'

Paama sat up slowly, moving as cautiously as if facing a lion who had just declared his intention not to pounce, but to have a friendly chat instead.

'Put on your boots and gather your things together. We are leaving. They will be after us soon, but I want enough time to present my case to you fairly.'

'Where are we going?' Paama asked with renewed anxiety in her voice.

'For now? Just a place,' he replied indifferently. 'Damp, slightly cold this time of year. We will not be there long. We must keep moving.'

Paama packed her new clothes into a neat bundle, all except for the boots and a grey woollen wrap. Those she put on, and, after leaving a few coins on the bed for the housekeeper, she stood nervously beside the indigo lord.

'What about you?' she asked as she examined his linen tunic and blue skin with doubt.

'No-one will see me if I choose not to be seen,' he said.

The feeling of moving from one space to another was almost pleasantly familiar by now. Paama watched his hand as he did it and wondered how it was accomplished. Then the sight of their destination drew away her attention once more. A light but persistent drizzle was falling when they arrived, giving a sense of overwhelming greyness to the land, sky, and everything in between. They were standing in the middle of a narrow, muddy street in a town. On either side, the buildings were fairly tall but irregular in their architecture and alignment. There was an uncanny quietness and a feeling of midafternoon in the featureless light.

'What is the name of this place?' Paama asked, squinting against the raindrops and pulling the wrap over her head.

The indigo lord, who was managing to keep himself and his clothes dry with his usual effortless power, paused before replying. 'Names are very important for humans, aren't they? How do I translate for you the name of this town as it seems to me, the true name that tells of its history and people and lands and weather and ... everything? Names have some meaning to humans, but names are *all* meaning for us, and we cannot translate them in a way that you will understand.'

'Do *you* have a name I could understand?' she asked and was surprised to hear the snappish irreverence in her tone.

It seemed to surprise him, too, but he rallied.

'No, I do not,' he replied haughtily. 'I will know when you are speaking to me, and you will have no reason to speak to anyone about me, so no name will be needed.'

'Then, O nameless one, tell me why you have brought me here.' She was beginning to understand why she was speaking so carelessly; she was tired of being frightened and growing increasingly angry that he had kidnapped her and was keeping her from her home.

He looked even more morose than usual. 'There is a plague in this town. That is why it is so quiet; this is a quarantined area. Only those who are dying remain here.'

Paama found fear again, and it silenced her. She barely heard him as he continued to explain.

'I want you to see why chaos is not a power that should be taken up lightly. You were proud of yourself that you saved a boy from drowning. Now see if you can help anyone here. Do you hear that sound?'

She strained and heard it. It was a man weeping loudly, certain there was no one to hear, his angry words mingling with wretched sobs. Almost absently, she began to walk in the direction of the sound until she came to a dark doorway with a door standing ajar. A stale, dank odour wafted out from the shadows into the fresher, rain-washed air of the street. It smelled as if someone inside had been sick and uncared-for for a long time.

Curious, but cautious, she pushed the door open with her foot and stepped over the threshold. The rooms were large and well-furnished, but everything was filthy with dust and litter. She walked on, drawing closer to the source of the noise. Finally she found it. In a back room with a small high window, there was a man on his knees beside a bed, and in the bed a woman, stick-thin, covered with ghastly sores, her chest moving with shallow, convulsive breaths as she slowly and painfully approached her death.

'A little story,' the indigo lord whispered in Paama's ear while the man kept up his loud wailing. 'She is a servant of this house. She remained free of the plague for a long time but was forced to remain and care for the sick. Then came the quarantine, and those of the family who were still able to do so fled by way of bribes and secrecy. This man is engaged to her. He has been seeking her for many days, and only today did he find a way to get past the soldiers who patrol the barriers. Now he comes in time to see her die, and soon he shall die, too, for they will not let him cross over again.

'Now, human Paama, what do you think you will do with your Stick?'

'There ... there is a chance that she might live, that they might both survive,' she whispered.

'There is that chance,' he acknowledged. 'Is that what you will reach for?'

She glanced at him, suspecting a trick, but his face was mildly curious and nothing more. Breathing scant in the fetid air, she kept her mouth closed and nodded.

'Then do it,' he said.

'Not as easy as it seems, hmm?'

'Leave me alone,' Paama whispered.

Her voice was hoarse from hours of weeping. It had not moved him, nor had it irritated him. He had let her cry without a word, without even a glance of contempt, but with an unexpected patience.

'I have left you alone for some time,' he said reasonably, 'but now we have to go.'

Drenched in rain and miserable, Paama got up from the doorstep, keeping her back turned to the house with its two bodies and its broken mirror. She scrubbed wearily at her ears, feeling as if she would never rid them of the echoes of the woman's screams.

'I didn't think she was strong enough to stand, far less reach for the mirror,' she mumbled, shuddering as her unrelenting memory stopped yet again at the moment when the woman used the shard of mirror glass to slice her own jugular.

Then her eyes widened in realisation and she turned on him with fresh energy.

'You knew. You could have told me,' she accused.

'Could I? There were many outcomes. There was a chance—a very slender one, I grant you—that they could survive here until the plague died out and the quarantine was lifted. There was a chance that she would recover and he would die later—such twists may seem cruel, but they exist. There was even a chance that they would both live and find a way past the quarantine barrier into freedom. There were thousands of chances. How was I to know that the one chance you needed to know about was the chance that she would see her reflection in the mirror and prefer death to a life of disfigurement, and that he would prefer death to a life without her?'

'So, your lesson is that one should do nothing without the knowledge of every possibility?' she asked bitterly.

'No. I only mean to show you that there are some chances that even the Stick cannot control—chances that involve the free will of a human soul.'

She thought about this for a while and then said sorrowfully, 'Then I might as well have done nothing.'

He flexed his hands uncomfortably in a manner that she was beginning to recognise. There was something he was not telling her.

'Was there something I could have done? Is there something I can do now?' she pressed.

He briefly clenched his hands into fists and then opened them in surrender. 'Before I... retired... I was assigned to burn this town.'

'Burn it!' Paama exclaimed.

He shook his head at her horrified look. 'It is the only way to stop the plague. Otherwise so many will die that the survivors will be forced to abandon the town entirely.'

'Then let us do it!' She did not even notice, in her enthusiasm, that she had said 'us' and not 'me'.

He shook his head again. 'It is too late. The rainy season has begun. Any fire I try to start will find sodden thatch above, soaked timbers and filled gutters below. It is too late.'

There was a strange expression on his face. It took her a few moments to identify it as guilt.

'Are you sorry that you did not do your duty?' she asked gently.

His eyes narrowed coldly. 'I am still not convinced that humanity is worth the effort at all.'

She looked hurt. Cold, wet, bedraggled, she must have made a pitiable figure, for he looked away from her uncomfortably.

'We must go now.'

She stood and stared at him, knowing he would feel not only the look, but everything behind it. It did more than she expected. It wore him down.

'There might be a chance, if the weather were dry for a few days, that a fire might still work,' he hinted.

'If I choose that chance, the chance of unseasonal weather, will you bring me back here in a few days?' she asked tentatively.

He nodded and then frowned as if annoyed at himself. Seizing her wrist again, he made an impatient motion with his hand. They vanished, leaving the street of the tragic plague town empty once more.

16

A RARE AND BEAUTIFUL THING

THE DJOMBI REMEMBERED THAT PAAMA had to eat, so they stopped in a busy, confusing, colourful metropolis where he could make himself visible without attracting very much attention. Paama found it necessary to pawn a gold coin to obtain the city's peculiar legal tender—colourful banknotes and dull coinage—before she could buy food at a small restaurant. While she ate, the djombi read from a newspaper and absently snacked on portions of her dessert ... 'just for the taste', he said. Paama recalled how fond another djombi had been of her sugar sweets and cakes, and she smiled slightly.

'We have a ship to catch,' he said at last, folding up the paper.

Paama found the statement interesting, but not as interesting as his action.

'Why do you read that? I thought that you knew everything,' she asked.

He seemed surprised. 'Where did you get the impression that I know everything? I do not know what you are thinking. I certainly do not know what you will choose to do next.'

'Except for my giving you the Stick. You seem very certain about that,' she said dryly.

He gave her one of his unfathomable, blank looks. 'I like to read the paper for the same reason that I like the occasional bit of food—to sample human tastes.'

'I thought you despised us,' she said quietly.

His hands squirmed on the folded newspaper. 'Not *despise*. Not all of human taste is abhorrent. There are bits that are enjoyable.'

'Like chocolate cake and comic strip humour?' she murmured, eyes downcast, sarcasm mild.

'Are you eating that last piece of cake?' he asked, unmoved by her criticism.

'That depends on what horrible thing you are going to show me next. I might need to fortify myself. Wouldn't it be more fair and balanced if you showed me something good about chance and human choice?'

'There is this ship—' he began.

'Please!' Paama cried, daring to interrupt. 'Answer me! Will you be fair?'

He seemed offended. 'I have every intention of being fair. I was trying to tell you, this ship will not be much to see at first glance, but there is something worth seeing, something rare. The point is, will *you* see it, or will you put the Stick to poor use?'

She pushed the remainder of the cake over the table towards him. 'Eat. I have lost my appetite. I forgot that this exercise of yours is not simply to show me how unworthy humanity is, but how unworthy I am.'

'There's no need to take it so personally,' he said, but he took the cake without any sign of remorse.

'No women on board,' he noted. 'I have given you a kind of invisibility. They will see you, but they will immediately forget who and what they have seen.'

He watched Paama struggling to stay upright on the surging deck.

'Try not to stumble into anyone,' he remarked. 'That's a little harder to forget.'

Paama doubted it. The crew members were busy. They moved quickly with the purposefulness of cogs who know precisely what is their place and function in the larger machine, but there was a touch of nervous exhilaration in their enthusiasm and preoccupation on every face.

'A storm is coming?' she guessed.

He nodded. 'Are you afraid?'

She set her face sternly and replied, 'I choose not to be, thank you. Are they all going to die?'

'Not all. Not even many. Watch.'

He found her a semi-sheltered spot, and she settled in with her back braced against the boards and her feet pressed against thick coils of rope. It was better to be seated, for now even the sailors stumbled from the motion of the turbulent waves.

Paama began to hate the djombi for his talent at keeping dry. For the second time in twenty-four hours she was drenched. Both salt-water and rainwater poured over her and pooled under her. She was thoroughly miserable and so self-absorbed that it was a shock when he spoke to call something to her attention.

'Look, by the upper deck.'

Lightning struck. Several men fell flat on their faces, some from the shock of the noise, but others actually stunned from having been too close to that massive surge of power.

'See that one?'

The djombi pointed. Whether he had been blasted up there or had fallen, Paama could not tell, but a man hung tangled in lines half-way up the mainmast, either dead or unconscious. She began to reach towards the bag at her waist for the Stick.

'Not so fast,' the djombi cautioned, holding back her hand.

'But he may be alive, and there's a chance that lightning will strike again before they get him down,' Paama protested.

'Trust me,' he said unexpectedly. 'The issue is not life or death this time. It's something more.'

Men were slow to move, still shocked by the force of the bolt of lightning, but one man, one sleek, wet, dark figure went climbing up the mast. A knife was held clenched in his maniacally grinning teeth, making him look like a pantomime pirate. He reached the hanging man, took the blade in hand, and drove it into the mast's wood before gingerly leaning out and catching a trailing line to haul the inert body towards him.

'Isn't that rare, isn't that beautiful?'

Paama looked back in shock at the djombi. His face and voice had never been so animated. He saw her expression and his face fell.

'You don't understand. You can't see it. Keep watching and I'll explain later.'

The rescuer pulled his knife free and began to cut his comrade loose from the tangled ropes. As he did so, Paama began to feel a sense of something about to happen, something beyond human capacity to prevent.

'No,' she breathed. 'I must stop it.'

'Paama, let it be.' His hand blocked hers gently, not forcefully, leaving her the freedom to shake it off and grab the Stick if she wished. 'Paama, *look at the boy.*'

Distracted, she looked at the young man he was pointing out, and thus never saw the moment when lightning, striking twice in the same place, blasted the two men from the mast. She did see the young man's expression. It was too intense, even when compared to the blaze of light that illuminated it. She felt seared.

The djombi began to speak quickly. 'The young man is the son of the man who was injured in the ropes. He has just seen his father's avowed enemy and lifelong rival give up his life to try to save him. This chance moment changes him for all time.'

'Didn't I hear you tell me before that you can't tell what people are thinking?' she snapped at him. 'How do you know he is changed? How can you claim to know the future which he will build out of his own choices?'

'I claim no such thing, but what I can see is how likely those choices will be, and I can tell you, Paama, many will be saved in the future when this man goes to war as a general because of this one time when he saw what it means to treat an enemy with love and honour.'

She heard his words but could not grasp that knowledge which allowed him to see the beauty in two more corpses, destroyed between fire and water. He realised. Once more he was at a loss; once more he looked at her with compassion, and regret.

The ship's crew began to recover their senses and rushed to their duties, removing the injured from the deck and striving with all their power to safeguard their own lives from the storm. It was over, and there were more things to be done—that was their way of dealing with it.

'I'm cold and wet and tired,' said Paama.

It was a bleak statement of fact, without any hint of a plea or complaint.

'I'll take you to where you can rest,' he replied.

He brought her to an empty tower high in the hills, a rest station used by hunters, in a country where the time was well past sunset. She was near collapse, wearied by constant travel, weakened by the elements, and grieved with loss. He put her to bed and set her to dreaming, and then went to the top of the tower to brood about his future.

Paama dreamed. If she had been able to bring with her the cushion from Sister Carmis, he would not have found her so vulnerable, but on this occasion, his influence and intent were benign, so we need not worry about her.

She dreamed that she was in a strange land of dry savannah and dusty winds. There were many people with her, all tired, all grieved, and they were made to march along an endless road to an unknown destination. Some fell and were dragged along by their comrades until they moved their own feet once more, preferring as yet not to die. Finally they arrived at a camp, a set of rough, ramshackle buildings made of bare, sand-scoured, heat-warped wood. It was the highest point from horizon to horizon, the only feature amid vast stretches of dry, yellow grass. Escape was made even less likely by the presence of guards whose faces showed that they blamed the prisoners as much as they blamed their superiors for their being posted to the middle of this barrenness.

The difference was that they could show their displeasure far more easily to the prisoners. Paama saw a woman pushed down by a guard for no other reason than that she was beautiful and fragile, and the guard, a hard-faced woman with the strength of a man, was tired of beautiful, fragile females who could not walk far or bear burdens without stumbling and fainting. As her husband stood powerless, held at bay by the weapons of other guards, the woman sprawled face down in the dust. The guard screamed at her and kicked the ground near her again and again, the heavy boot coming closer and closer to her flinching body. Paama could no longer bear it. She rushed at the guard, beating her down to the same dust, and stood with her heart pounding at her folly, expecting to die.

There was no reaction, only the sound of slow, firm footsteps and the snap of booted heels coming to attention. She turned to see a man in a drab but neat uniform walking towards her. He stopped and looked at the two women on the ground, the prisoner and the guard, and at Paama standing between them. There was a long silence. Then he stooped and lifted the prisoner, put his arm about her, and helped her to her husband's waiting arms. To the fallen guard he gave one uncaring glance, and with another glance he dispersed the other guards. The last look was saved for Paama, and it was a long look, and only the intensity of that look identified for her the face of the boy who had looked into the lightning and seen death ... and something else.

All right, she thought angrily in the midst of the dream. *I understand now, I see it. Not with the beauty that you have seen, but I grant you your vision. Now leave me alone and let me rest!*

The dream ended. If the remainder of the night held any more dreams, she did not remember them.

He had the nerve, the following day, to ask her how she had slept. She narrowed her eyes at him and did not answer. The taste of dust was still in her mouth, the brawling yells of the guard echoed in her ears, and the look of the man's eyes remained printed on the back of her mind.

'Wherever you plan to take me today, I do not care, but I tell you I am tired of death and crisis. If you cannot show me something lighthearted, I will kill myself and save you the trouble of ever having to convince me to return your power to you.'

He blinked, slightly startled. 'Lighthearted?'

'Yes,' she said firmly. 'Entertain me. Have a thought for my sanity. Perhaps your kind can look long at the deep questions of existence, but our sort need variation in our philosophical diet.'

He pondered briefly. 'I could show you the tricksters at work.'

'And who are they?'

'Minor adversaries. Sometimes they must be stopped, but at other times they are allowed to do their worst. I can show you tricksters who have been permitted to teach someone a lesson.'

'This will be entertaining?' she asked doubtfully.

'Some humans find it so. There will be no death, I promise you, but there will be severe embarrassment, which is but a small death of the ego.'

Paama shrugged in resignation. It sounded as if that was the best compromise she could expect.

'Give me time to have breakfast, and then we can go.'

17

THE SISTERS IN CHARGE, AND THE TRICKSTER IN TROUBLE

THE SEARCH FOR PAAMA AND the indigo djombi was still on. Sister Elen watched diligently every day and sometimes at night and wrote down everything that she could see. Sister Deian hovered beside her in case there was anything to tell Paama. Sister Carmis worked the hardest, spending hours upon hours in sleep or meditation. She said she was looking at probabilities, but they had become too varied and numerous for her to find anything meaningful. Instead of following a few bright threads in the fabric, she was caught in an irregular, brilliant, dynamic web.

'Not very informative,' she admitted, 'but still rather exhilarating.'

The other searchers were moving with equal blindness, arriving at places moments or hours after their quarry had left. If the djombi had pooled resources with the Sisters, they might both have gotten somewhere, but the djombi didn't think to take human abilities seriously, and the Sisters, knowing little about such beings, didn't imagine that it was even possible to collaborate with djombi, so they were both the poorer for it.

However, when humans must rely on their own powers, they can be immensely resourceful. Sister Carmis put the idea out into the open by telling the Sisters of a dream she had had of a warrior-hunter seeking Paama's trail.

'That's it,' said Sister Jani. 'We'll hire a tracker.'

'Not from around here,' warned Sister Elen hastily. 'I think we should not alarm Paama's family just yet. We need to keep our actions secret.'

'Ahani is the place to find good trackers,' Sister Jani remarked. 'No-one asks your business there.'

The Sisters nodded, and then an awkward silence fell. None of them wanted to go to Ahani. Makendha supplied most of their needs, and on the rare occasion that something additional was required, it was sent for.

'There is something else that concerns me,' said Sister Carmis. 'We saw the truth of what happened that night, a truth that no-one now seems to recall. The poet Alton appears to be content to be a lord, and Neila is willing to marry him, but what of that man, the major-domo, who once more pretends to be so ordinary? I do not trust him. I would be happier if he were out of Makendha.'

'How are we to accomplish that?' asked Sister Elen. 'I might Read him from a distance, but if I dared to speak to him face to face, I might lose my memories and my purpose in an instant. His master may have put protections on him, the same as he did for his poet.'

'Then we deal with him from a distance,' said Sister Deian.

'We will send him a message threatening him with exposure,' said Sister Jani, her eyes flashing. 'Let him try to modify the memory of an entire town full of people after we tell everyone who he is.'

'Wait,' Sister Carmis said, frowning. 'He might know something about where his former master is going. Shouldn't we try to bargain with him first?'

'Who knows if these people have any sense of honour?' Sister Elen sighed. 'We need something to bind him to be obedient to us, at least for a while.'

If the Sisters sound rather daring in their plans, it is because they did not really know who they were dealing with. Although their memory of the evening was untouched, their perception of what had happened was awry. Both the Trickster as Bini and the indigo lord in his disguise as Alton had shown but slight signs of something changed in appearance. Alton, on the other hand, had been almost entirely controlled by the indigo lord so that he could have the demeanour of a lord to match his own gift of eloquence. He had shown so much influence and interference swirling about him that Sister Elen had Read him as the most dangerous, and Sister Deian had pronounced him the centre of the entire disturbance.

The confused scenes that had followed had been made even more obscure by the darkness and by the peculiar effect of the time bubble, which did not easily permit sight at a distance. They knew that Bini the majordomo was deeply involved in the conspiracy to get the Stick and the subsequent cover-up, but they had not yet grasped the fact that he was not human. Out of all the three, Sister Carmis was the only one who had the slightest idea of his true nature, but unfortunately she had taken her dreams of spiders to be as symbolic as her dreams of the visible web of probabilities.

Therefore the Sisters are plotting something that would work very well for a human, but that will have unexpected consequences for a djombi.

The Trickster was treating himself to a sort of holiday. He was going to establish Alton permanently as Lord Taran, preferably in a residential district just off Ahani so that Neila's nouveau riche tastes could be satisfied, and then he was going to hand in his resignation and go back to his usual haunts in Ahani. As for the real Lord Taran, the Trickster didn't spare him a thought. He had seen enough. Getting between half the host of undying ones and one fallen comrade would be going to a level of danger that he was not accustomed to. Danger for the sake of fun, that he could appreciate, but unreasonable risk taking was not part of his character.

So comfortable was he in his vision of his likely future that the note that came down from the House of the Sisters via the postboy was quite a shock. Humans had seen him and remembered him? How was that possible? He would have to start paying closer attention to the little toys and gadgets that were so popular in the larger cities, and that now, apparently, had come to the hinterlands as well. He read the first part of the message more closely and realised that they had not, in fact, seen *him*, but that he was guilty by association with the indigo lord. He crumpled the note in his hand. There was a simple answer to this problem. He would hand in his resignation a bit earlier than planned, and Bini would disappear, his face never to be seen again in this country.

He raised the crumpled paper in his fist and laughed as he shook it in the direction of the House of the Sisters.

Grant him this one theatrical moment. It is going to be of extremely short duration.

His laughter choked off as he saw before him not a human fist, but the sharp-tipped, bristly leg of a spider. He blinked in horror and tried to reassert his image, but nothing happened. The postboy, who had been waiting in case an immediate reply needed to be sent, stared at him in frozen terror.

The Trickster pulled himself together. 'There is nothing to worry about,' he told the boy as reassuringly as he could manage. 'These things happen. Just run along and deliver the rest of your letters.'

Other powers remained intact, for the postboy paused in confusion, nodded peacefully, and then went off to complete his work.

The Trickster gnashed his mandibles in irritation. The power over memory worked best when used on those whom one would rarely see. It was perfect for large and busy towns or cities, and for short interactions, but in a small village like Makendha he would end up having to destroy the short term memory of half the inhabitants to sustain his disguise.

He smoothed out the crumpled note and read it through carefully with a feeling of grudging admiration. Not many people managed to trick the Trickster, but when they did he was willing to give credit where credit was due. Well, he was not going back to Ahani without his secondary power of disguise intact. With a little less elegance than his previous employer, he waved a forelimb in the air and stepped through the crack in space and time—out of his own tent and into the House of the Sisters.

Sister Elen was the first to see him. She started to scream, but he raised a leg wearily.

'This is all your doing, so don't fuss. Who do I have to deal with to get my disguise back?'

She stared at him. 'Deian!' she yelled.

The Dreamer came running. On her head was a cap made of the same fabric that covered the cushion she had given to Paama. The Trickster looked at her and observed the immunity to mind tampering.

'No need to be so defensive,' he said, trying to make soothing gestures with his forelegs, and failing miserably. 'I realise that perhaps you didn't know what was beneath the disguise when you decided to block my power to maintain it, but now I'm sure we can both agree that it would be better for all concerned if I looked a little less . . . intimidating.'

'Where's Paama?' demanded Sister Deian.

'I honestly have no idea. I'm not really involved. Trust me, none of my kind would wish to get caught up in this matter.'

He was afraid that they would think he was lying, but, both

Dreamer and Reader looked at him, their faces showed disappointment at the truth of his words.

'But that has nothing to do with me. Won't you let me have back my disguise?'

Sister Elen had the pained expression of someone who was thinking very very quickly. 'You have to agree to leave Makendha and never return again.'

'Never?' he said, dismayed.

'Never,' she reiterated firmly.

He nodded, pretending to be resigned, but secretly he thought that there were always ways to get around 'never'.

'And since you and your ... kind cannot—or will not—help us find Paama, you must go to Ahani and hire us the best tracker you can find,' she went on bravely.

'I can do that,' he acknowledged. 'And you will let me have my disguise back, so that I can carry out this mission?'

'No. You can have it back only when the tracker reaches the House and is approved by us,' said Sister Elen.

'And has found Paama,' added Sister Deian.

'You bargain shrewdly. You must have heard about me before,' he smiled. Unfortunately, this movement showed itself as an ominous clicking of the mandibles, which caused the two Sisters to jump back in fear.

'No, no, I will do as you say. I will find you a tracker and stay in Ahani. You can return my disguise to me from a distance?' he asked pleadingly.

'Yes, once the terms are all met,' said Sister Deian.

'Agreed, then.'

The spider-man backed away cautiously so that no sudden move of his might startle them, waved a foreleg gently in the air in farewell, and vanished.

18

THE SPIDER IN HIS PARLOUR AND A VERY EAGER FLY

AND SO WE RETURN TO a familiar scene—the spider-man sitting in a bar, observing and choosing his victims. If his seat was a little farther back in the darkness than usual, and if the bar was less cheerily lit than his previous haunts, we can understand why. He was a little nervous about having no disguise to fall back on.

The thought crossed his mind that he did not have to put up with this. Although he had long borne the spider shape, he could yet retire it and craft a less remarkable shadow. It would take a little time to do it, but the change might do him good. Perhaps … perhaps indeed it was time to put aside the legend of the Trickster with one last trick.

Then he relented. Better to start a straight trail with an honest deed.

Other honest deeds had been faithfully carried out. Alton's writings, the first part of a great work, had been sent by courier to an agent. Neila's orders for fabric and other wedding paraphernalia had been delivered to the appropriate stores, and the goods were being shipped directly to Makendha. Alton's household was being managed by a temporary majordomo, a junior looking for advancement hired from the chief's staff in Makendha. He thought it was temporary, but the Trickster knew that a permanent offer was just around the corner.

The Trickster sighed. All he needed was for one more thing to go right.

The first adventurer he approached with a free drink (alcohol definitely helped his situation), was a big man of middle years who had recently suffered an injury and was trying to return to full marketability. The spider-man recognised another trickster when he saw one, and this man was hiding the fact that he had lost his nerve after the accident that had nearly maimed him permanently. It was a common characteristic among the warriors—no fear of death, and only pride for their scars, but little thought of all that could happen in between those two extremes.

Then there were a few who were more brag than bravery, youngsters who had little or no experience who were travelling the world to find themselves. There were others who, having unfortunately found themselves, were seeking a way to get lost again. All these the Trickster turned away. He knew something about the business of tracking, and it required single-mindedness, not self-absorption.

Precious days were lost in this way, and he began to think that perhaps it was time to be less picky. Then, at last, the perfect tracker found him. He was a thin man of medium height, with light scars tracing his left cheek just below his eye. There was an expression of muted amusement on his face, as if he thought he was part of some grand joke and was glad of it. The Trickster found his face naggingly familiar, which was surprising, because he knew he had never met him before. But we have met this stranger, oh yes, a long trail back. More than mere coincidence had brought him to the Trickster. Certain information had come to him, making him realise that there was unfinished business on his karmic plate.

'You've been looking for me,' he proclaimed to the spider-man who, as usual, had tucked himself discreetly into the darkest, farthest corner of the room.

Then he added audaciously, 'Aren't you going to buy me a drink?'

'That depends,' said the Trickster cautiously. 'Who told you I was looking for you?'

The newcomer shrugged. 'There are many answers to that. I could say that the word is out in Ahani that someone is sifting through the city's entire allotment of trackers to find the very best. In fact, I think that is the best answer for now.'

And he made a small, elegant gesture with his hand as if to say, 'your play'.

'It is true that I am looking for a tracker, an excellent tracker. The assignment is no ordinary quarry,' the Trickster murmured, signalling to the barman for an extra glass of spirits.

The tracker caught the barman's attention and signed for water instead. The Trickster didn't know whether to be impressed or worried.

'In what way is your quarry unusual?' asked the tracker.

The Trickster's eyes gleamed with pleasure. This would be enjoyable.

'It leaves no trail. It can travel from one end of the earth to the other in the blink of an eye. Oh, and did I mention it has the powers of chaos at its side?'

'What does that mean, exactly?' asked the tracker, as if only slightly curious.

'It means that if there is a chance of your getting lost, or run over by an omnibus, or hit by debris from a falling star ... well, you'd be surprised how easily those chances can get called up when your enemy has the right tool to hand.'

'So, it sounds as if I shall have to be careful that this quarry does not suspect I am following,' mused the tracker.

'There is more,' the Trickster snapped. 'There are others on the trail ...'

'... the nonexistent trail,' the tracker interjected helpfully.

The Trickster glared at him. 'Exactly so. There are others, as I was saying, and it is best that you do not try to get between them and the quarry.'

'When I do track down the quarry, assuming there is nothing stopping me from doing so, what am I to do then? Return it to you?'

The Trickster relaxed and leaned back. Here at last was the enjoyable bit. 'That is not my concern. I have been instructed to hire the best tracker Ahani has to offer. More information on your duties will have to come directly from your employers.'

'My employers. So, I have got the job?'

The Trickster inclined his head in assent. 'Why not? Time is short and I am tired of looking any further. Here is a ticket to Makendha. You will have to find your own way from there to the House of the Sisters, but you can hire a mule from anyone and go up the hill trail. But before you go . . .' and here he gripped the tracker's hand just as it was reaching for the ticket, enjoying the sight of the slight swallow in the man's throat as he dealt with the experience of being manhandled by a giant spider, '. . . what other reasons would you have for thinking I was looking for you?'

'Why do you ask?' The tracker's face was less cheerful now, more anxious.

'You do not discuss wages, or deadlines, or reasons for the assignment. You do not flinch at any of the strangeness in my words nor even my appearance, and I know this for a fact because I have long since lifted my pacifying influence from you, the mental sedative I use to keep humans from curiosity and wonder and fear. Who are you? What is your name? Who sent you?'

'I am a tracker,' the man replied in a quiet voice. 'My name is Kwame, and . . . and I was sent by a dream.'

There was a small silence.

'A dream?' said the Trickster, releasing his hand and letting him take the ticket. 'Well, I wouldn't doubt it, with all the nonsense that's been happening lately. A dream. Why not. Anything to make my job easier, thank you, Sisters. Once I was the strangest thing around here, the Sultan of Weird, but now the humans are outpacing the weird ones. Such is life.'

'You must not let yourself become cynical,' chided Kwame. 'We only do what we can, and sometimes we are permitted to do even more than that, human or ... otherwise.'

The Trickster gave him a measuring look. 'You are a philosopher, I see. And yet young. What has made you so wise before your time?'

Kwame shrugged. 'I try to pay attention to life's lessons.'

The spider-man laughed. 'So modest? Let me tell you, I have seen men who are trying to find themselves, and I have seen men who are trying to lose themselves, but rare indeed is the man who knows exactly who he is and where he is at. Kwame, I sense that you are that fortunate and rare man.'

'I thank you for the compliment, but in truth I am trying to find a part of myself, something that I lost on the way from childhood. My dream tells me that at the end of this quest is where I will find it.' A smile quirked at the corner of his mouth. 'Finding out that someone like you is at the start of it is oddly encouraging.'

He drained his glass of water and stood up. 'As you said, time is short. I will go to the House of the Sisters and do as they command me.'

The Trickster watched him go, relief spreading like a narcotic to his extremities, removing that unconscious tension that had burdened him since reading the Sisters' note. He had done his duty, his conscience was clear.

Conscience? he asked himself. *Have I really slipped that far?*

He dropped some coins on the table, snapped himself briskly out of the bar with a click of his pincers, and went to visit a friend.

'I thought you might still be here. Not off chasing with the rest of the grand hunt?'

His friend, who wore the shadow of a woman, had made herself remarkable by the glowing silver of her hair. Otherwise, she appeared to be simply a woman. I can admit to you now that this is the senior djombi who sent the Stick to Paama. Her reply to his offhand salutation was calm, and cryptic.

'I find that sometimes if you just sit still, things have a way of finding you before you can find them.'

The Trickster tried to process this, shook his head, and returned to the issue of his inner struggle. 'You have ruined my reputation, do you realise that?'

She looked at him affectionately. 'You were ready for ruin, do you realise that?'

He shrugged, which can be a lovely thing to see when six out of eight shoulders are going at once. 'Ruin has even less of a future for my kind than it does for yours. People are quick to believe in a fall, but how often do they acknowledge redemption?'

'My poor friend. Are you really worried about what all your former comrades will say? Or do you think they will believe you are carrying out the ultimate Trick, to infiltrate the enemy?'

'Lies are impossible between us. They will believe it, and they will not be kind.' He sighed and twiddled his pincers sadly. 'Sometimes I wish I could simply disappear, and let only the legend remain.'

'What an excellent suggestion. Why don't you do just that?'

He gave her a baleful look. 'If you have a bright idea, please do share it with me.'

She smiled, and did so. When she finished telling him, he was smiling too.

19

PAAMA MEETS ONE OF THE MASTERS OF RIDICULE

IT WAS EARLY MORNING. THERE was a chilly precipitation somewhere between a very light rain and a heavy mist that muted the rich greens of the valley with a veil of grey. The djombi looked pensive as he led Paama through long, wet grass. As usual, he was completely dry.

'It must be nice, not to have to eat, or sleep, or get cold and wet,' Paama complained, shaking the drizzle off her grey wrap.

'It must be nice,' the djombi parroted in reply, 'to taste, to dream, to feel the wind and the rain in your face.'

Paama gaped at him. It was the most complimentary thing she had ever heard him say about being human. 'Do you really think so?' she said in a small voice when she was finally able to speak.

'I am only pointing out that everything has its advantages and disadvantages,' he said.

'And yet you can taste food . . . when you choose,' she pointed out.

'When I choose,' he admitted.

'What are your disadvantages?'

He continued to walk smoothly through the grass, leaving a silvery trail for her to step into.

'Duty,' he said at last, a single, glum word.

'We have duty, too,' Paama countered.

'Not like ours. You're weak, and allowances are made for your

141

weakness. There's forgiveness for you. Mercy. I don't see why, personally.'

'I know. You think we deserve to be left to perish in our own self-made misery,' she accused.

He did not answer at first, but then he said, 'I thought you wanted this time to be lighthearted. You're not making a very good start of it.'

She kept silent, kept her head down, and looked at the rain-silvered grass instead of at his back. In this way, the sight of the mansion came on her all at once, looming out of the grassy plain like a small citadel of pale stone. There was a tidy skirting of lawn around it, hemmed in by stone walls topped with wrought iron.

'Where and what is this place?' she asked.

'We are near the capital of your own country. This is the country house of a wealthy statesman who retired to spend more time with his wife and young son. However, his wife often grows bored—it's very isolated here—so he takes her to more exciting places. They are visiting the capital right now.'

'And the boy?'

'Here, of course. There are servants enough to take care of him, but of course a servant is not a parent. He has too much of his own way.'

'He sounds like Ansige,' muttered Paama.

The djombi turned to her, his eyebrows raised in query.

'My husband,' she said, and was ashamed to have to say it. 'Now we live apart, but when I was in his house . . . oh . . . he had grown up spoilt and he wanted to continue spoilt. He almost drove me mad. I was ready to kill myself until my parents hinted to me that I still had a home to return to.'

He was staring at her so fixedly that she felt even more ashamed for having revealed this sordid part of her past.

'Never,' he said flatly, 'never speak so easily of killing yourself. You have no idea what that means.'

And he turned away from her and walked off, leaving her baffled and abashed at the stern rebuke.

Just then there was a shriek, and a side door opened so abruptly that it slammed against the wall and almost bounced itself closed again. A woman dressed in a simple servant's uniform came leaping over the threshold with a broom in her hands, vigorously swiping at some small and undesirable vermin which moved so quickly that it was a mere scuttle leaving a wake of shivering grass blades. She danced in fury and brandished the broom even as it fled.

Paama ducked down behind the wall and peeked through the iron bars at the scene. A little boy, about eight, came charging out from behind the servant with such speed that she spun in place like a panel of a revolving door.

'That's my mouse! Don't you dare kill him!' he yelled at her, and flung himself on the lawn, trying in vain to grab the small creature.

'Your mouse? *Your* mouse?' she screamed. 'Then what business did it have in *my* apron pocket? You're a bad boy, Jevan, and only getting worse. If you don't mind yourself—'

'You'll tell my parents?' he finished coldly, pausing in his search to sit up and glare at her. The haughty expression on his face showed just how much contempt he had for such a threat.

The woman's eyes narrowed dangerously as she realised she was being mocked. 'If you don't mind yourself,' she began again deliberately, 'if you don't learn to control yourself, the baccou will steal your skin and behave so badly that even you will be ashamed of yourself!'

He got up and ran, yelling over his shoulder, 'I wish it would!'

Just as Paama was shaking her head and smiling ruefully at the little tyrant, a deep, sorrowful voice behind her made her jump.

'There's my cue. Duty calls. But how strange to see you here . . . and with a human, too. Duty for you as well?'

A fuzzy, undefined shape was hovering before the djombi, who was looking slightly embarrassed. 'Not quite duty, but essential nevertheless,' he replied.

'Ah,' the newcomer said diplomatically and did not press the matter further. 'Well, if you've come to see my work, the best view will be from inside the house in the playroom, the boy's bedroom, and the kitchen. But for now, watch outside.'

The shape suddenly blurred the insubstantial air, rushing towards the boy, who was still racing around the house in an excess of furious energy. There was a soft, soundless collision.

'Ow!' the boy shouted, more from shock than pain.

He opened his eyes wider and raised his hand to his head. Surely he had damaged himself somehow, for there was his own self, sitting on the grass, also rubbing his head and looking at him with mischief.

'Didn't really hurt, did it, you crybaby?' his image told him callously.

Fright set him on his feet. 'What are you?'

'You, of course!'

'No, you're not! You're that baccou that Hana's always talking about.'

'Who's the baccou? I can see right through you!'

It was true. The boy looked down at himself and saw the grass growing under the soles of his feet, and then he glanced up at the impostor, who was solid, and real, and twice as cheeky and wild.

'Go away!' he shrieked, nearly in tears.

The baccou stuck out his tongue. 'You called me, so I'm not going till I've had my fun. You can watch if you like.'

With that, he raced inside and banged the door shut. The poor faded youngster scrabbled at the doorknob uselessly until he realised that he might not be able to grasp a doorknob, but then again, he could walk through the door. As he disappeared inside the house, the djombi led Paama through a short space-time step that took them directly to the playroom. The baccou was already elbow-deep in the toy box, and the boy was hovering about frantically, unable to lay hands on anything.

'Good loot,' the baccou commented, throwing things out carelessly and banging things together as if testing them for durability. 'More than birthday presents and Christmas gifts in here. How in the world do I do it?'

His foot found a tiny wooden train and deliberately stamped it into fragments.

'That's *mine!*' the boy howled in horror. 'Stop smashing my things!'

'Don't be silly, *I'm* smashing my things. I can do that, can't I? From what I remember, I do it all the time!'

'Give me back my skin!'

'Jevan, what are you doing up there?'

'Oops,' said the impostor. 'All yours.'

And he walked through the shade of the boy, leaving him tangible again, and tucked his fuzzy shadow into the corner next to Paama.

Steps came thundering up to the room and Hana burst in like vengeance. '*What* have you been doing?'

'It wasn't me!' came the automatic wail from the boy. In a room apparently empty of anyone but himself, the plea carried little conviction.

'Go to your room,' she ordered and was shocked to see how quickly he ran out of the playroom, almost as if something was chasing him. If she had known the significance of the weird blur that followed him, she would have realised it was true, but she merely rubbed tiredly at her eyes and muttered something about the boy raising her blood pressure.

The djombi brought Paama to the boy's bedroom just in time to see the boy thrashing about on the floor, fighting the baccou for his skin again.

'Leave me alone!'

'Not till I've had my fun!'

The baccou won, naturally. He began to pace around the room, looking for something to break while the boy's shade followed him, all but wringing his hands in impotent anguish.

'Leave that, it's my—no, don't *touch* that! You'll smudge the—hey!'

'Ohhh, what's this?' The baccou paused in front of an aquarium. It needed cleaning, but it was vivid with iridescent, colourful fish.

'No,' the boy whimpered. 'Not my fish.'

The baccou shrugged. 'My mischief's very person-specific. I won't hurt them. But you have to admit I should have cleaned it out by now.'

He looked around, grabbed a cup from the bedside table, dumped the contents of a vase out of the window, and then carefully transferred the fish to the vase. As he lifted away the last of the fish, he carelessly tapped the side of the aquarium with the vase's heavy base. The pane of glass splintered and the cracks began to ooze liquid.

'Slow leak,' remarked the baccou. 'Ah, I'm wrong,' he corrected himself as the rest of the glass finally gave way, deluging the floor with water and weed.

Hana was at the door as quickly as if she had snapped her fingers and whisked through space-time. 'Now what? Oh ... *no!*'

She scrambled out and returned with a mop and pail. Yanking the vase away from the baccou, she carefully poured the fish into the pail while fending off the spread of the water with the mop. Then she began slopping in the weed angrily. The boy's shade danced about her, trying to get her to see his plight, but she ignored him and turned instead to the grinning baccou.

'You,' she said through gritted teeth, 'get out. No dinner for you.'

The baccou rushed out of the door, muttering, 'Kitchen. Better stock up now while I have the chance.'

The boy let out a screech of fury and frustration and ran after him. Paama found herself grinning as she went with the djombi to the third observation point. How many times had she thought that if only Ansige could see how he appeared to others, he would be desperate to change?

The baccou was tearing messily through the larder, throwing food down and smearing his face with flour, molasses, anything that would stick and look ridiculous. When the boy saw him, he sat down on the floor and wept helplessly until the baccou stopped his rampage and squatted down beside him, a sympathetic expression on his face.

'It's not so much fun anymore, is it?' he asked the boy softly.

'N-no,' the boy sobbed.

'Well, it's not fun for me anymore, either. Call me up again if you want me, but you can have your skin back now.'

Then there was only the boy, sitting in a mess on the floor, his face and clothes dirty. He hiccupped once, looked around with scared eyes as if waiting for something to pounce, and then crept out of the room.

'That's done,' said the baccou with satisfaction, back to his indistinct form once more. 'Seems a ridiculous job when you think about it, but some derive benefit from the exercise. But you had a question?'

He rounded on Paama, who was taken aback at first, but then she bravely spoke her thought. 'I was just wondering, does it only work for children? It's just that ... well ... I've got this husband, Ansige ...'

The shape flickered in a manner that somehow seemed apologetic. 'Ansige the Glutton? I'm sorry. No-one's going to be assigned to him. Not much time left there.'

Paama was stunned by the pang of fear and worry that shot through her bones and drained her of strength. 'Not much time?'

'I'd go visit if I were you. Anyway, can't hang around. Another call is coming through. Toodle-oots.'

And with that, he vanished.

Paama sat weakly on the nearest chair. 'Ansige?' she said softly to herself.

'Tell me where he lives,' said the djombi quietly. 'I'll take you there now.'

20

KWAME MEETS THE SISTERS AND BEGINS THE HUNT

KWAME WAS NOT ALLOWED ANY farther than the courtyard of the House of the Sisters. The four who had hired him sat before him on a long wooden bench, looking far too much like a tribunal.

'A woman is missing,' said Sister Jani.

Kwame was an experienced tracker. That meant that whatever the Trickster had told him had been temporarily set aside so that he could listen to what the Sisters had to say without making any assumptions.

'Describe her to me.'

The Sisters looked at each other, and then Sister Jani answered, 'She has courage. She has braved scorn and ridicule, which can tear the soul more viciously than vultures at a corpse. She has managed to keep her self-esteem intact.'

'She has compassion and discretion,' added Sister Elen. 'She does not pull down the weak, and the secrets of others are safe with her.'

'She has integrity,' continued Sister Deian. 'When she goes about doing what is right, she does not consider solely her own benefit.'

'She has the most beautiful dreams,' concluded Sister Carmis on a wistful note.

Kwame listened politely, and then he coughed even more politely. 'I meant, what does she look like?'

The Sisters appeared to be slightly taken aback.

'Medium height?' hazarded Sister Jani.

'Slim build, hair braided in spiral style...'

'A rather long nose...'

'But really very ordinary to look at.'

Then Sister Elen sat up straight. 'She was wearing a brooch in the shape of a dragonflower, though she may have put it aside now.'

'And a headband in bronze-coloured material...though she may have taken it off,' mused Sister Deian.

They fell into a glum silence. Sister Elen was fretting, wondering how she was going to work into the conversation her knowledge of the places that Paama had been without betraying the arcane methods by which it had been acquired. Sister Deian was brooding over their lack of proof. The brooch and the headband no longer functioned, having succumbed at last to hours of being drenched by rain and saltwater. And yet, even if he believed them, the House of the Sisters had secrets that were not to be told to lay persons.

Kwame detected the lull and tried to get them to talk again. 'What was her occupation? Before she disappeared, that is?' he corrected himself. Referring to a client's loved one in the past tense was never a positive approach.

'She was a marvellous cook,' smiled Sister Jani. 'She had skill in her hands and love in her heart, which is the way to make food fit for the angels.'

'Did she work at a restaurant? A guest lodge?'

'She was here with us, last,' said Sister Deian sorrowfully.

'Do you know why she has disappeared?'

Again that silence fell, so odd to a stranger, so understandable to us. Kwame looked at them with greater and greater suspicion.

'Perhaps I should ask some questions down in the village,' he suggested, raising an eyebrow.

'Oh, don't do that!' Sister Jani cried. 'Her own family doesn't know—they still think she's with us!'

'That's very interesting,' said Kwame levelly. 'Why haven't you told them?'

'We didn't want them to worry,' said Sister Carmis, and twitched visibly at the weakness of her excuse.

'Nevertheless, if I am to find her, I need something more than what you seem prepared to tell me. It would be better if you allowed me to ask my questions. I can play a role—pretend I am simply a restaurant manager looking to recruit a cook—and they will not learn from me that she is missing. Would that satisfy you? If it does not, I tell you frankly that I will not be able to do anything for you.'

They looked at him in dismay.

'Very well,' said Sister Jani. 'Go and ask your questions. We will confirm your ruse if you wish. But we ask only one thing. After you have heard from the villagers, return to us. We will have more things to tell you, things that may appear strange, but are no less true for all that.'

Her colleagues gave her slightly anxious looks, but she stared directly at Kwame and pretended not to notice them.

Kwame inclined his head in thanks. 'I shall do as you say.'

The village court of Makendha, like village courts the world over, was sometimes graced by the presence of an itinerant storyteller. Kwame found one sitting on a stool under the shade of the sandbox tree, muttering to himself. He knew the type. He found them to be excellent observers of humanity, professional harvesters of gossip and scandal.

'Excuse me,' he said, approaching the old man, 'but I am trying to find a cook by the name of Paama.'

The old storyteller ceased his muttering, turned his aged and weathered face to Kwame, and gave him a good look up and down.

'Now, there's an accent that has walked far,' he said.

'I have no accent,' Kwame replied.

'Ah, that is how I know it has travelled so far, to have wrapped itself in so many layers that to everyone, no matter what region they hail from, it appears you have no accent. So, you are looking for Paama? Why?'

Kwame had few qualms about lying for the sake of his profession, but something about the twinkle in the man's eye—little short of a leer, it was—made him embarrassed for no good reason. He scuffed his foot awkwardly in the dust and said, 'A good cook is always in demand, and her fame has spread beyond the village.'

The wrinkles on the old man's face assumed a less satyric aspect as he folded his hands and sighed.

'I have heard tales of how magnificently she can cook. I could relate for you a description of a morsel of her honey-almond cake, a delicacy which is light enough to melt on the tip of the tongue and yet it lingers on the palate with its subtle flavours long into the dream-filled reaches of the night. I could sing the praises, second-hand, alas, of her traveller's soup, a concoction of smoothly blended and balanced vegetables and herbs guaranteed to put heart and strength back into the bones of the weariest voyager. I have heard of her pepperpot, wherein meat from the hunt simmers slowly all the day long in a fantastic chutney of seasonings, selected spices, peppers, and green pawpaw. And forgive my tears, but I have just this moment recalled a certain jar that sits in her kitchen, filled with dried fruit steeping in spice spirit, red wine, cinnamon, and nutmeg, patiently awaiting that day months or even years hence when it will be baked into a festival cake that will turn the head of the most seasoned toper.'

He sighed again and stopped for a moment. They both swallowed at the thought of such culinary genius.

'Pardon me for raising what must be a painful subject, but it sounds as if you have not tasted Paama's cooking for yourself,' Kwame noted.

'You are too perceptive. I have indeed missed the golden years of Makendha. My business requires me to travel, and it seems to me that whenever I am away, Paama is cooking here, and whenever I return, she is cooking elsewhere. It is a cruel trick of fate, but I pray it shall soon be ended.'

'What is your business, if I may ask?' Kwame inquired.

It was best not to appear to pry too openly, and the subject of self was always a welcome change. As he expected, the storyteller was happy to talk about his work.

'I am a storyteller. I travel to collect stories, and I return to tell the stories of one place to the people of another. That is the important part of the trade. You must never tell people their own stories. They have no interest in them, or they think they can tell them better themselves. Give them a stranger's life, and then they're content.'

'But the court is empty now . . .' Kwame pointed out.

'Of course it is. Do you think that one simply spouts off before an audience, impromptu and unprepared? I was rehearsing for this evening's performance. But we digress. We were speaking of Paama and her cooking.'

'Yes,' said Kwame, glad that he had returned to Paama without being prompted. 'Perhaps you could tell me where I could find her, so I could ask her about her experience.'

'Haven't you been listening? These days, if I am in Makendha, it is almost a guarantee that she is not.'

'But someone must know where she's gone,' Kwame insisted.

The old man shrugged. 'I can tell you nothing about the matter.'

'Then I am wasting my time,' Kwame murmured, using the slightly forlorn look of a man who has travelled far for little benefit.

It seemed to work, for the storyteller continued. 'Never mind. Keep searching for her; she is worth the finding. She will be an asset to any restaurant. Already she is accustomed to cooking for twenty at a time . . .'

'How so? She has operated her own restaurant?' Kwame asked.

He chuckled. 'Nothing as lucrative as that. She has had a huge mouth to feed, a real belly-beast to pacify. But surely you have already heard the tale of Ansige the Glutton?'

Kwame shook his head, no.

'Well, since you're a stranger and thus entitled to the tales of this village, I'll tell you.'

And he told Kwame the entire tale of Ansige.

The day after that, Kwame returned to the House of the Sisters. His face was very still, as if he had heard something that had provoked such a strong feeling in him that he could not risk letting any sign of it show in his features. When the Sisters saw him, they realised that something was very wrong.

'Why didn't you tell me about what happened to her husband?' he demanded.

They looked a little surprised. They had not expected that the tribulations of Ansige were at all relevant to the search for Paama.

'We didn't know it was that important,' said Sister Carmis.

Kwame closed his eyes as if gathering patience. 'When a woman goes missing after first leaving her husband and then being left by her husband, no matter how strong her ability to face gossip and speculation, I think that it might be a factor in her disappearance. When the husband has been publicly ridiculed, I grow even more suspicious.'

Eyes thus closed, he did not catch the frantic look exchanged between the Sisters, who knew just how off the mark he was.

'I will go and question this Ansige,' he declared.

'But—'

'I would not be at all surprised if he knew where she was.'

'Wait a mo—'

'In fact, I would not be surprised if she were with him right now,' he continued.

'There's more to it than—'

But Kwame was already striding through the gate and back down the trail, his destination now certain.

Sister Carmis was the only one who recovered herself in time to dash after him and say, 'But there's more we have to tell you! There's more to this situation than meets the eye.'

He stopped and smiled at her. 'You're the one who dreamed me, aren't you?'

She nodded shyly. She was the youngest of the Sisters, not yet confident in her skills, and hesitant to wield authority.

He touched her arm gently in reassurance. 'Trust your dreams. Perhaps there's more to *me* than meets the eye.'

Waving a farewell to the House of the Sisters, Kwame set off to begin his hunt for Paama.

21

PAAMA COMES FULL CIRCLE AND LEARNS THE DJOMBI'S LESSON

THE VILLAGE WHERE ANSIGE LIVED was nearly large enough to be called a town. The main street was busy, but the crowd was not yet so anonymous that Paama felt comfortable with the idea of sauntering up to the front door. Respecting her desire for discretion, the djombi brought her to the back garden of Ansige's house. She stood for a while staring at the grounds in silence.

'Do you want to go back, Paama?' the djombi suggested gently.

Pity from a being so pitiless made her feel angry, though she could not understand why. She muttered something about the herb beds being overgrown and then walked with a grim face towards the back door. As she raised her hand to knock, a loud voice came from inside the house.

'You ate an hour ago! The doctor said you should not be eating so often—'

'I pay you to prepare my meals, not to repeat some quack's words in my ear!'

Paama's breath caught in her throat. The first voice was unknown to her, but the second voice was only just recognisable as Ansige's. It was weak and querulous, ten years aged in sound.

The first voice, which was closer to the door, was heard to mumble that no amount of money could be worth the aggravation of standing watch over a man intent on eating himself to death.

157

'Are you going to bring my food to me or not?' Ansige demanded.

Paama wondered if the servant could hear the edge of fear in Ansige's voice. *He must really be in a bad way if he cannot even come to the kitchen himself.*

There was a cacophony of crashing, cursing, and stamping, and then the door flew open so suddenly that Paama had to leap back to avoid being struck. The person attempting to come through the door reared back in shock.

'Who are you?' he demanded.

'His wife,' Paama replied, startled into directness, giving an upward jerk of the chin to point in the direction of the unseen Ansige.

The man's face went sombre. 'God help you,' he said bluntly, and pushed gently past her, striding to the back gate with the utter determination of a man who has reached his limit.

'What is the matter with him?' Paama called, but he only flapped a hand behind him in exasperation and went through the gate without bothering to turn around.

She stepped inside the kitchen and looked around. Tumbled pots and broken dishes testified to the cook's last spasm of rage, but there was a large pot intact on the stove, its still-bubbling contents puffing out the scent of broth. Even beneath the recent destruction, the large kitchen appeared untidy, as if one servant had been forced to do the work of many. Paama cleared away some of the debris and searched the cupboards until she was able to put together a tray with a bowl of soup and a plate of bread.

The passage was unswept, the bannister of the stairs dusty and laced with cobwebs. The door of the master bedroom stood ajar, and it resisted slightly when she pushed at it. When she entered, she saw why—clothes were strewn on the floor. Ansige was lying in bed, his face turned to the wall as if sulking.

'Hello, Ansige,' Paama greeted him.

Ansige's head turned slowly until their eyes met. 'Paama. You've come back to me.'

She couldn't bear to correct him. She simply brought the tray over to the bedside table, set it down, and said, 'I heard you weren't well.'

She hated the sound of her own voice. It was a dead sound, lacking emotion, the kind of voice used when talking to someone so close to death that it makes no sense bothering them with details. She had heard doctors using that voice when visiting terminally ill patients. And Ansige *was* ill. For all his complaining, when he reached for the tray of food he moved slowly, as if in pain. Then he began to eat the soup, and Paama felt wretched. His mouth made hungry motions towards the spoon as it came closer, but his chewing and swallowing were feeble. Now she better understood the disarray in the kitchen. His mind was, as always, hungrier than his body, and it made him call incessantly for meals that he was physically incapable of finishing.

'The house seems empty,' she remarked.

Ansige's mouth twisted bitterly. 'Cheats and thieves and sluggards, all of them. I can barely get a housekeeper to come in twice a week, and the cook is just a disaster.'

Paama said nothing, but she recalled that she had left a house that supported seven servants—five full-time and two part-time.

At last his hand wearied, and he dropped the spoon into the half-full bowl with a sigh. She quickly took the tray from him as his body slumped tiredly.

'Just a quick nap,' he mumbled, and fell asleep in seconds, curled up tight like a foetus refusing to leave the womb.

She put the tray down again and sat in a chair by the window. She had not noticed before that the djombi had left her, but now she thought about him and how vindicated he would feel to see Ansige's self-destruction. This was truly the bathos of human experience, a gift of life and opportunity squandered and spoiled. The image of the baccou crossed her mind, and she frowned. Why should she be so quick to blame Ansige? Not all the undying ones were altruistic in their actions. She braced her hands on the arms of the chair, about to get up, but fell back in surprise. The djombi was now in the room and standing beside her.

'You do come when you're called, don't you,' she said sourly, though softly, so as not to wake Ansige. 'I have a question for you. What's wrong with Ansige?'

He stared at her, not understanding. 'He is dying.'

'I know that,' she snapped. 'For years, until I tired of it, I told him he would wear out his body by eating so much. What I need to know is *why*. Why was he constantly eating? Was there more to it . . . did something influence him to behave as he did?'

His expression was almost pained, as if she had asked something she shouldn't have, but he walked over to the bed, looked at Ansige, and then put his hands wrist deep into Ansige's belly. Ansige did not stir, not even when the djombi withdrew his hands with a sudden jerk. There was a small, shadowy blur cupped in his palm.

'How long have you been here?' he asked it.

The blur flickered. 'Not as long as one might think. Not as long as *she* thinks.'

There was a slightly malicious tone in its words. The djombi looked sternly at it until its self-satisfied glow faded.

'Who else has been here?' he queried.

'Several others,' came the sullen reply. 'None stayed for very long. I'm the only one lazy enough to enjoy this, and frankly it hasn't been fun even for me lately.'

'What does it mean?' Paama asked, careful to stay in her chair on the opposite side of the room.

The blur seemed to perk up again. 'I mean he's worse than weak.

He's in love with his vices. One can't suggest anything to him. He has the thought already, and the mere idea that someone else is thinking it too is enough for him to act on it. Most of us can't stand that—no challenge—but, like I said, I'm lazy. I'm content to sit back and watch the show.'

Paama turned her face to the open window and put her hand over her eyes. So much for her most recent theory on Ansige's gluttony. Poor Ansige; he was not even able to blame ill influences for his shortcomings. It seemed unfair that the djombi was right, that humans were largely responsible for their own misery. Even more than unfair, it was ironic that he had taken her the wide world over to prove his point when he could have simply brought her here and shown her what remained of the man with whom she had spent ten years of her life.

When she looked back at the djombi, he was carefully rubbing his hands together, as if crushing something out of existence.

'Could I use the Stick? Is there any chance that he might live?' she asked. Even as she said it, she knew she was asking as a formality, for the sake of decency.

The djombi dusted his hands and considered for a while before replying. 'For how long? For days, definitely. For weeks, maybe. But longer? You know the answer already, Paama.'

She stood up, took the Stick out of the cloth bag at her waist, and gave it to him. Although his hands reached for it automatically, he hesitated just before his fingers touched, his eyes questioning her.

'I think you can take it safely,' she reassured him, then added with a hint of bitterness, 'Both my heart and my hands return it freely.'

He nodded, and took it from her. The universe did not even blink at the momentous transfer.

'I ask one thing only,' Paama continued. 'Go back to the town with the plague, and burn it.'

His left hand briefly gripped the Stick, and then held it out to her again. For a moment she thought, afraid and bewildered, that he was refusing to do what she asked, but he said, 'Take back the stick. I don't need it. I have taken the power that was in it.'

She took it out of his hand. Did it feel different, lighter? She couldn't tell. She looked up at him, and realised something *was* different. Though not yet fully at peace with himself, he was whole now, and if she looked closely enough, she thought she could make a guess at his name . . .

'You won't come with me?' he asked.

She looked at the sheet-covered heap that was Ansige. 'No. I will stay here and take care of him. He won't be as much of a bother to me as he was in the past. Go now, before the rains start again and it is too late.'

'It won't matter. I can move in time as well as space when I am by myself.'

'So, you could go back and do all your duty at the appointed time? You could come out of "retirement"?' she hinted.

'Yes, I could,' he agreed, acknowledging only the possibility.

He looked down at Ansige, apparently troubled about something, perhaps struggling with what was, in effect, good-bye.

'If it is any consolation to you, he would not have lived any longer if you had stayed with him,' he said awkwardly.

Paama looked hard at him until he looked back at her, so that she could show him how her face was part smiles, part tears, part guilt, and part relief.

'Now I believe you when you say you cannot read my mind. Hurry up and go. I think he is waking up again.'

22

SOMETHING POSITIVE FROM A GRAVE MISTAKE

WHEN HE RETURNED TO THE streets of the quarantined section of the town, someone was waiting for him, someone silver-haired.

'Hello Chance,' she said.

'Hello Patience,' he replied cautiously.

Mere nicknames, shadows of the whole appellation even as their visible, tangible bodies were shadows of the self in its entirety. But I must do what I can for my human audience.

'You are alone.' It was a statement—it was clear she was alone; but it was also a question—*why?*

'The others stopped hunting for you the moment you left Paama alone. I . . . well, knowing the schedule of duty, I knew where you would be.'

He said nothing. It was no surprise to him that his unconscious, untold decision should already have been announced to the universe.

He glanced down the street. There was a thin spiral of smoke rising from an upper floor window in one of the deserted houses.

'Unless you want to walk through flame, we should leave soon,' he remarked.

She shrugged. Fire would not harm them, but assembling a new shadow took time and energy. They began to walk away from the thickening smoke.

'What changed?' she asked him.

He walked a few more pensive steps, and then answered. 'Paama is an unusual woman.'

There was a distant crackle of timber burning. The two looked back and saw that an entire upper storey was suddenly fully ablaze.

'Liquor stores,' Chance remarked, and the two continued walking.

'Not as unusual as you might think,' she said, replying at last to his comment about Paama. 'There are many women like her, considered by some to be virtuous and loyal, considered by others as foolish and weak. What about Paama changed you?'

'Nothing stopped her from trying to do what she felt to be right, not even despair. She was willing to learn, and when she felt the lesson was beyond her capacity, she was willing to simply obey.'

'Ah, so you saw her duty,' Patience said, sounding pleased.

'No. Not at first. She saw her duty long before I noticed it. There are many things that I once knew but which I had forgotten, and one of them was that human duty is not very different from ours.' He sighed, and changed the subject slightly. 'So, what will my punishment be?'

'Yes, I expected that. Once your despair had run out, the pride would come forward. What kind of punishment would make you feel you had properly paid your debt? What degree of severity would allow you to feel superior to others who had transgressed and been let off more lightly? Be careful what you answer.'

He felt hurt. 'I only speak of the correct order of things.'

'Crime and then punishment, I know. But what is the purpose of punishment?'

He paused for a long while to consider this. It suddenly struck him that he was being tested. 'To restore the one who has erred to the former position of trust and authority.'

'To wipe out the fact of your disobedience? Try again,' she scoffed.

He mused a while longer, feeling small and slightly panicked as he did so. 'Payment? Restitution?'

'And again you speak of things that will clear your debt. Suppose your debt can never be cleared. What then?'

'Are you telling me I will never be allowed to return to my work?' he asked, aghast.

By then they had crossed the quarantine barrier, but the blaze was not far behind. It blew forth a hot wind that had alerted the barrier guards to the growing danger, but they were hesitant to act, debating whether saving the city from swift death by fire was worth risking a slow death by plague. As miserable as Chance was feeling, he paused for a moment with Patience to watch their agitation.

'There is a chance that they might decide to simply restrict the fire to the quarantine area,' Patience noted.

'There is a very large chance that they will try and fail to do so. Look above!'

There were glowing embers flying in the air like small firestars, each one bearing the contagion of disaster over the quarantine barrier.

'Let us walk forward,' Patience suggested, and the pair took one giant step through folded space into the centre of the city.

It was still very peaceful there, the peace of a Sunday morning. There was a faint sound of music which was louder than the clatter of the scant traffic in the streets. Although it was neither his concern nor his duty, Chance felt some relief. Fewer people meant that there would be fewer to fight the spread of the fire, and it also meant fewer victims. The cloud was a smudge on the horizon, partially obscured by high buildings, but it was beginning to loom and darken the day. Curls of ash were already being chased through the dry gutters by the wind.

Patience was humming softly. '*Redemption* by Lewis, I believe. How very appropriate. You were saying something about being allowed to return to your work? Chance, not very much has changed. You met one woman who shamed you into returning to your duty; later you will encounter hundreds of more common souls who will drive you to such frustration that you will again neglect it. Should you be allowed to return to your work?'

Chance kept silent and let his steps drift closer to the sound of the music. It was coming from a small, domed theatre. He stopped in the portico and peered inside. The audience was hushed and intent, as devout-seeming as any congregation hearing a bishop's sermon. The vocal orchestra was a dim blur at the back of the hall, but even at that distance there was something in their faces that showed through the faintly smoky air.

'Redemption and mercy for them, but not for us,' he murmured.

Patience sighed. 'You are being so difficult.'

They stood for a while listening to the music, much of which sounded familiar, while the sky darkened and ash spiralled down from above. Finally, the sound of snapping, crackling flame joined with the vocal harmonies, and smothered coughing began to be heard in the crowd.

'We've stayed too long.' Patience stepped out of the portico and pointed to the dome of the theatre. The dry wind had carried embers far in advance of the main blaze, and there was an ominous, dense smoke pouring down from the roof.

Inside the theatre, a rumbling of worried noise began to rise above the music.

'Time to go, I think,' Chance said. 'Shall we go forward, or leave?'

'Neither. Let us go ahead a few days, then a few months to see how the city has recovered.'

Just as the junior djombi had put his hosts into bubbles of slowed time, so did this senior pair spin around themselves a cocoon from which they, open eyed, were able to see a sudden bloom of flame and smoke, the microsecond collapse of the dome, and then a lingering haze.

'Go straight on,' said Chance, changing his mind. 'I want to see it rebuilt rather than burnt.'

They went ahead so quickly so that all outside was blurred twilight, and then they slowed to check the state of the ruined theatre. All the wood was gone, but the stone walls and pillars stood like blackened monuments to the devastation. Thus it remained for quite a while, but then at last there was evidence of clearing and cleaning. Chance and Patience watched with interest as the frame of the dome was raised and the dome itself billowed up around it as if the very shingles had feet of their own to scurry into place.

Finally, the images beyond the transparent barrier steadied. They pulled aside the veil of time and looked out but stayed partly on the threshold of their own world.

'Less timber,' Chance commented, looking around at the new architecture.

Patience was too busy examining the schedule of performances affixed to the theatre door to pay attention.

'*The tragedy of Olen and Mara, a sung play in three acts,*' she read. '*Based on a true story of the Great Plague.*'

'Typical,' Chance said in tones of deep depression. 'Give them a crisis, and they must turn it into a form of entertainment. Do they really remember what happened here? People died, people killed themselves rather—'

'—rather than live on without beauty and love. Yes. It's all here in the play's summary.'

'Is it?' He went to stare at the schedule, and an odd expression came over his face, as if he were unsure whether or not a smile was called for. 'Paama's star-crossed lovers are now immortal. I wonder if that would please her.'

'Something positive from a grave mistake,' Patience mused. 'Yes, I think that would please her, if she ever found out.'

Chance did not reply. He knew that contact was limited between humans and the undying ones for good cause, but at that moment it was yet another thing to make him feel miserable.

She noticed, of course. 'You miss her.'

'Time means nothing to our kind. How could I miss her?'

'Because she is not where you are in either time or space, that is how. I think this unusual woman has done more than shame you. She has taught you something about how to be vulnerable.'

He looked at her angrily, but she raised a hand in protest.

'I did not say "weak". I said "vulnerable". Is that such a terrible thing?'

He subsided, but only slightly. 'Not terrible, no, but it is just another word used to describe the human condition.'

She shrugged. 'Your opinion. But we have strayed very far indeed from the topic at hand. We have to decide what is to be done with you. Restitution is beyond your ability; redemption is, in your opinion, not an option for our kind; so I offer you a third possibility—rehabilitation. You are too valuable to waste. Why not take a period of time to properly learn the lessons you have merely glimpsed over these past few days?'

'I cannot believe it would be so simple.'

'Of course it wouldn't be simple. It would be hardship, suffering, every kind of testing and privation. It would certainly not be a holiday. At times it might even approach restitution, but you must remember that it is not; it is a gift, a second chance.'

Chance looked at her and considered long and hard. He had tried isolation, and it had been sterile and useless. He had tried to do as he pleased with humans, and instead of senseless vermin he had found Paama, remarkable in her own ordinary way, and very burdensome on his conscience. He found himself running out of choices.

He bowed his head, and said humbly, 'What would you have me do?'

'What you are already doing. Trust in more than your own power. I have shown others the way to redemption, and I can show you.'

He seemed sad for a moment. 'I suppose I will have to give up the power of chaos again.'

'Give it up for the first time, you mean,' she laughed at him. 'I had to take it from you by force to bring you to your senses. But yes, you will have to give up that and many other things as well. But I promise you, I will keep all these things in trust for you until you return. Are you ready?'

He was afraid. He realised as she stared at him that she was far more senior to him than he had ever realised, far more senior than any of his kind that he had known, but that she was only now allowing him to see the full extent of her power. Still, he had little choice but to trust her. He closed his eyes and offered himself, and felt her gently wind his powers away from him like silk from a cocoon, leaving him unshielded, weaponless, and naked.

He shivered. He had never known such weakness, such fear of annihilation.

'What happens next,' he whispered, still not daring to open his eyes.

She gathered him into her arms until he felt warm again, and even safe, and then she said, 'You must be born again.'

23

ONE DOOR CLOSES . . .

FINDING PAAMA WAS EMBARRASSINGLY EASY. Once Kwame entered the main street and asked for the whereabouts of Ansige's house, a passerby wordlessly pointed him towards a large stone and wood structure whose open door was swarming with humanity. Some of the people appeared to be in either great distress or great happiness—it was difficult to tell which. Kwame drew nearer with some hesitation—he disliked crowds.

There was a man sitting on the pavement a short way off from the door. His face, which bore an expression of poignant woe, was partly hidden in his hands. Kwame sidled up to him, unsure as to whether he should intrude in the man's grief.

The man lifted up anguished eyes and thought he saw a comforter.

'I knew this would happen,' he said 'I knew it, but would he listen? Of course not.'

'Ahh, my deepest sympathy, but can you tell me—'

'Giving credit is no better than gambling, gambling on a man's honour, gambling on a man's good luck. But he said that it always paid to do business that way with the lesser chiefs and their kin. What did I know? I was only following orders! But he'll make this my fault somehow,' he concluded bitterly.

Kwame added his knowledge of Ansige to the man's words and tried a guess. 'You are a grocer?'

171

'A junior partner in a wholesale grocery company,' he confirmed, and then his face fell into deeper depression as he added, 'but not for much longer, I fear.'

'I am sorry, but can you tell me where I might find Paama, Ansige's widow?'

The grocer jerked his head towards the door, saying with a weak smile, 'Good luck getting through. I understand only the undertaker's been paid so far, and that's because thirty degrees and eighty-percent humidity is kind to no corpse.'

Kwame managed something between a grin and a grimace in reply and started towards the door. After a few steps, his stride faltered. It was bedlam. People were pushing each other out of the way; the moment someone shouldered their way in, they were almost trampled by someone storming out.

'This is not my way of doing things,' Kwame muttered to himself.

He bypassed the entire drama and slipped down a side alley. It was walled off at the end, but there were green, leafy branches hanging over a corner of the wall, hinting at gardens beyond. He climbed the wall and discovered a small footpath that led to another road, but he ignored that, choosing instead to jump lightly down into the adjacent garden. The divisions between the back gardens were low and flimsy, so it was only a matter of a hurdle, a quick sprint from an angry dog, and a rolling dive over a fence before he was in the back garden of the late Ansige's residence.

The gate there was shut up tightly, just as he had expected. Paama was sitting on the back doorstep with a knife in her hand and a bowl in her lap, trimming string beans. She froze and stared at him warily for a second before throwing the knife into the bowl and scrambling up hastily.

'Sister Jani and the others sent me,' he explained quickly, getting to his feet and spreading his hands to show he was harmless.

'How do I know that?' she challenged, hesitating on the threshold.

'Sister Carmis dreamed me. And I see you're still wearing your headband, but I don't see the brooch.'

Paama slowly relaxed, or at least became less tense. 'I should have sent a message to them when I got here,' she admitted. 'But first I was taking care of Ansige, and then this...'

Shifting the bowl into the crook of her elbow, she rolled her eyes to indicate the noise of the ongoing mayhem at the front of the house.

'That's Ansige's lawyer they're tearing apart. I had to give him a good portion of my gold before he would agree to settle the debts and the estate for me. I've done what was expected of me, and I don't want to do any more.'

'Didn't your husband leave you anything?'

'Anything that wasn't already collateral for a greater debt? No. I suppose they will have to sell off the house to pay off everything. No matter. I wouldn't have wanted to stay in it anyway.'

'Will you be coming home, then?' Kwame asked.

Paama's mouth twisted. 'I must stay for the funeral at least. That's the last of my duty. Then back to the House of the Sisters to tell them my news and to Makendha for my sister's wedding. After that, who knows?'

Kwame nodded. 'I know. Sometimes grief can only be cured by wandering. I have done it myself. Then again, I have often wandered for the sake of wandering, so I suppose it would be hard to tell the difference.'

She smiled. 'Wandering for the sake of wandering. I like the sound of that. But tell me, young man, do I *look* grieved?'

He paused and examined her. 'You look tired ... a bit fed up, which is understandable given the descent of the vultures ... and a little bit sad, but not as if bereaved, though. As if you are missing something. Or someone.'

She did not lose her smile, but whatever humour or cheer there had been in it seemed to fade out, as if a cloud had dimmed the world.

'Something or someone indeed, and possibly both,' she replied. 'And neither of them are Ansige or anything to do with him. I left him more than two years ago, and there was plenty of time for me to finish my grieving then.'

She seemed to shrug to herself, as if pushing an old burden off her shoulders. Then she looked at him sharply. 'How did you know to find me here? As you have already noticed, I had to set aside the brooch a while ago.'

'I guessed,' he said simply. 'I asked questions, I made assumptions and I acted on them. I believe the Sisters thought I was very impulsive, though.'

She raised her eyebrows in surprise. 'It was a very good guess. Did the Sisters tell you why they thought I might be elsewhere?'

Kwame shook his head, amused at the memory. 'I think they tried, but getting information out of them was like extracting gold from ore—a lot of labour and time, and why bother to do it when you know there's a store just around the corner? I figured that if I was wrong, I had at least eliminated the obvious, which is the first duty of a tracker.'

She smiled again, this time with more brightness. 'I'd say that chance brought you. The obvious would not have helped you in this situation.'

Then, without warning, she began to cry.

There are a few men in the world who are unmoved by tears from a woman. Kwame was not one of them, but at that moment he wished very much indeed that he were. He came up to her, without a handkerchief, without anything useful and soothing to say, and patted her arm with clumsy concern.

She started to laugh through her tears, which unnerved him even more.

'I am so sorry. It's just that I've had a very . . . strange time recently. Are you a good listener? I don't even know your name, but it would help if I could talk to someone.'

He smiled. 'My name is Kwame, and in my type of work, one *has* to be a good listener.'

She sat on the doorstep again, set the bowl in her lap and absently returned to her previous work as she told her tale. Kwame leaned against the door post and watched her as she talked. She told him the whole story of how the Stick had been given to her and how her life had been transformed thereafter. From time to time she glanced at him anxiously to see if disbelief or scorn was showing on his face. Kwame did not have to dissemble. It was no hardship for him to keep his face calm— except for when he looked stern at the cruelty of the indigo lord; awed at the story of the bandit treasure hid beyond human reach; sad at the plague deaths; stirred at the sailors' courage and the general's integrity; and amused at the naughty little boy who learned how terrible a thing it can be to be beside oneself.

In fact, he reacted in much the same way as I hope you did when you heard it for the first time—and perhaps even more so, because although Paama did not have a storyteller's skills, she had the advantage of having been the one to suffer through the tale's adversities first hand. Kwame listened and felt for her. Compassion is a great amplifier of empathy, and at times it is the only thing that can make a dull story interesting.

When she finished speaking, he remained pensive and silent, so silent that she grew embarrassed.

'Well . . . it is not an ordinary tale . . . no doubt you think me mad,' she said, awkwardly trying to laugh while her knife flashed and nipped off the last of the string beans in a fury of desperation and chagrin.

'I think it is indeed an extraordinary tale,' he agreed, and then he looked straight at her with eyes that did not judge, and continued, 'I also think that you are an extraordinary woman.'

The knife hung immobile for a moment as they stared at each other. Then Paama blinked and bent her head over the bowl, drawing her fingers repeatedly through the mass of beans to see if any were left untrimmed.

Kwame cleared his throat. 'Perhaps I can send a message to the Sisters on your behalf?'

'Yes, thank you. That is something I must do at once,' she said.

But she did not get up, and he did not move from his position by the door post.

'If I may,' he said tentatively, 'it might be a good idea for you to have someone about. The lawyer has enough on his plate, and I fear that others may try to harass you.'

'Yes,' she acknowledged sorrowfully. 'I would feel safer with some-one else about, but I don't want to drag my family into this. They have already suffered from my marriage to Ansige, and I ... well, it might be foolish, but if I could spare them this last bit I would be thankful.'

He shook his head. 'You don't have to trouble them. It would take a while for them to travel here, perhaps too long. I was referring to myself. After all, I'm already here, and if you have any concerns you can ask the Sisters about me ... they can vouch for me ...'

'Oh,' Paama said, and she looked lost and deeply disappointed. 'I ... thank you, of course ... but I have to be careful. I have to watch my money—I wouldn't be able to pay you for your time.'

Kwame looked very serious. He knew instinctively that he had to be very careful what he said next, for a woman's sense of honour and pride and independence was in many ways no less fragile than a man's.

'I wouldn't worry about that if I were you. I've already been hand-somely paid.'

24

THERE IS NOT MUCH MORE to tell. Paama was the principal mourner at a poorly attended funeral. The worth of Ansige's property was enough to cover the debts, but the crafty lawyer played the claimants against each other by promising swifter consideration of their claim if they paid him a large enough stipend. In reality, he dragged out the process for far longer than was necessary. Paama quickly extricated herself from the situation by formally relinquishing all claim to any part of Ansige's estate, and returned to Makendha.

We have already heard her immediate plans—debriefing the Sisters, attending her sister's wedding—so let us travel through time and skip the boring parts. Let us go forward a year or two and see what is happening in Makendha.

When a young man marries a recently widowed woman a few years older than himself, eyebrows are knowingly raised and tongues wag. However, when an enterprising, up-and-coming young man with a successful tracking business marries a poor widow whose worthless husband has left her nothing, not even children to take care of her in her old age; and when said widow happens to be one of the most amazing cooks to be found the length and breadth of the entire continent . . . well, then people mutter enviously about the sheer luck that some people have, and move on to something more scandalous so they can gloat happily over another's misfortune.

Naturally it was Neila who thought she had made the prize catch with her merchant prince, who had by now retired from business and was making a fortune with his published poems. And, to tell the truth, Tasi and Semwe were thoroughly relieved that they had married her off so well to a man willing and able to treat her in the manner to which she thought she was entitled. Yet parents always have their secret favourites, and while Alton was the one that outsiders oohed and ahhed over, Kwame was not only their son-in-law, but the son of their heart. His steadiness and his dedication to Paama proved him to be everything that Ansige was not, and Tasi gave thanks daily that her prayers for her daughters had been answered with such accuracy and to the benefit of all concerned.

Kwame combined his savings with the remnants of Paama's bandit gold and built a house on the edges of Makendha, halfway between the House of the Sisters and Semwe's residence. However, a small village like Makendha could not provide enough work and challenge for a master tracker. Soon he was travelling out to get work and Paama, who was still interested in seeing new places, started to accompany him. Tasi was worried at first, but Paama promised her that they would return often, and that when grandchildren came, they would all settle permanently in their Makendha home.

Did Paama ever see a djombi again? It is certain that she kept her ability to ignore the whispers of the tricksters, and perhaps she was a little more aware than most of the reasons for someone seeming a little stranger than usual, but she did not see such marvels as in those few days of madness when she held the power of chaos. As for Kwame . . . you may think that he had only been humouring her when he listened to her tale, but in truth he did believe her. Paama never spoke of it again, but the habit of trust was well established after that heavy proof, and never was it broken.

One of the enjoyable parts of travelling was that Paama was able to visit the places she had seen so briefly before. Sister Elen was able to deduce the names of almost all the towns and cities she had seen by matching their appearance with current events—or, in the case of the raided town, history. The only place she had not seen was the house where the baccou-ridden boy lived. As for Paama's dream of the prison camp in the heart of the savannah, she and Sister Carmis agreed that it might be a dream of a possible future, and it would be better not to probe it too deeply. Savannah land was all too common in their country, and the idea of a coming war was comfortable to no-one.

So Paama got to walk through the town that had endured the plague and the fire, and even saw the *Tragedy of Olen and Mara* (and yes, she guessed who and what that was about). Though she looked and looked, she could not find the street she had known in the former quarantine area, because the fire had changed all but the greatest landmarks.

She even got to sail on a ship, fortunately in far better weather. The city where she had watched the djombi eat chocolate cake and read the newspaper was on the other side of the world, but Kwame had been eager for the adventure. The oasis with the ruined town was almost as difficult to get to, but worth the challenge. Kwame wistfully asked her whether she could remember the spot where the djombi had taken her underground to get the gold, but shifting dunes had already changed the landscape and they were forced to travel on, enriched by experience rather than treasure.

Kwame used his time, talent, and opportunities wisely and set up a network of junior trackers so that he was able to delegate work and take contracts farther and farther afield by using his foreign connections. Paama worked as a cook wherever they went, and even when she started off in a small restaurant, she would usually end up the private chef of some rich noble who would pay her extravagantly to stop her from going to work for anyone else. They returned to Makendha periodically for vacations, and they used their money to quietly improve their modest home and its surrounding lands.

As promised, they came back permanently when their twin sons were born, a fortunate decision, for Semwe passed away a few years later, victim to a seasonal fever that was often fatal to the old and the very young. Much to Paama's surprise, Neila invited their mother into her household in the suburbs of Ahani, and Tasi went willingly . . . perhaps to bribe her with the promise of free caregiving if only she, too, would provide her with a grandchild. Their childhood home was rented out until it would be needed again, and Paama took over the lands and livestock.

I cannot think that you would need to know much more about Paama's life after she gave up the Chaos Stick. You may, however, want to know more about what happened to Chance, and Patience, and the Trickster. I could tell you, I suppose, but humans are the proper study of humankind. Why should I encourage you in this inappropriate interest in beings you cannot fully understand? Let us just say that the Trickster entered the equivalent of a witness protection programme. He would emerge at a time in the future with a new identity which would protect him from the suspicion of his former adversaries and any possible retaliation from his former allies. Chance underwent rehabilitation for a similar period of time, and Patience watched over them both, but from a distance, visiting only occasionally. Senior as she was, she delegated the day-to-day observation of her charges to someone else, someone who had proven skills in the field.

Now I have come at last to the end of the story. For some in my audience, a tale is like a riddle, to be solved at the end. To them I say the best tales leave some riddles unanswered and some mysteries hidden. Get used to it. For others the tale is a way of living vicariously, enjoying the adventures of others without having to go one step beyond their sphere of comfort. To them I say, what's stopping *you* from getting on a ship and sailing halfway around the world? Tales are meant to be an inspiration, not a substitute.

Then there are those who utterly, utterly fear the dreaded Moral of the Story. They consider it an affront to their sensibilities and a painful presumption on the part of the storyteller. They are put off by the idea that a story might have anything useful to say and, as a result, all the other joys a tale has to offer them are immediately soured. I save my most scathing remarks for them. Do you go through life with your eyes blindfolded and your ears stopped? Everything teaches, everyone preaches, all have a gospel to sell! Better the one who is honest and open in declaring an agenda than the one who fools you into believing that they are only spinning a pretty fancy for beauty's sake.

I was honest and open. Don't you remember? I told you from the very beginning that it was a story about choices—wise choices, foolish choices, small yet momentous choices—for with choices come change, and with change comes opportunity, and both change and opportunity are the very cutting edge of the power of chaos. And yet, as the undying ones know and as humans too often forget, even chaos cannot overcome the power of choice.

I have no way of knowing which of these characters will most capture your attention and sympathy. Paama will be too tepid and mild a heroine for some; they will criticise her for dutifully caring for her estranged husband in his last days. Chance will be too cold, the Trickster too odd, Patience too distant. In stories as in life, it is an impossible task to please everybody. But before you dismiss them, I ask those who care for the weak to look at Patience and see their own professional distance, so essential for maintaining their own strength amid the trials of many. Look to the Trickster to see your eccentricities, your talent for mercy deep-hidden underneath a fearsome exterior; to Chance for your self-centredness, self-pride, and despair; and to Paama for your sense of familial duty ... and yes, I think I can get you to admit that you may not like my people, but you cannot fail to recognise them.

Do I have more stories to tell? There are always more stories. I could tell you about how Giana grew up and became a famous choreographer who captured some of the dance and movement of Dreamland for the waking world. I could give you the amusing tale of what happened when Neila and Alton did finally have a daughter. And then there are sadder, more serious histories, like the account of the general's war, or the not-always-lucky and terribly volatile adult life of Jevan, the boy who met a baccou. I can give you any tale you like, and some that you might not like, but which would still be to your benefit.

And yet ... it is terribly dry and thirsty work, speaking these lives into the dusty air of the court, speaking for you to hear and ponder and judge. Perhaps, if you would be so kind as to contribute, I could purchase some refreshments now, find a place to rest my head later, and return to you on the morrow with my voice and memory and strength restored. Please, ladies and gentlemen, if you have at all enjoyed my story, be generous as the pot goes around, and do come back again soon.

Epilogue

I HAVE BEEN AUTHORISED TO add this epilogue to the tale. Not only is this in order to placate that demanding portion of my audience who felt that to end with vague hints of Paama's married life was to end too abruptly, but it is also to round off the story according to my own rules. I have been hoist by my own petard, constrained by that offhand statement: *the proper study of humankind is humans.* So be it.

Imagine then two humans, boys, aged about twelve years, sitting in a primitive treehouse. It lacked walls, there was no roof—in fact it was more of a treeplatform than anything else, but imaginations that can make castles out of the air can certainly build marvels on a few planks.

'She knows,' said the elder twin smugly. 'That's why you're her favourite, admit it.'

'How can you be sure?' his brother replied, looking far too serious for a boy his age. 'I know she worries about me. She's constantly afraid that I'll get hurt, or that people will laugh at me, but that's just her way of protecting me. It doesn't make me the favourite.'

'Trust you to see the sunny side of things,' came the exasperated reply. 'If I weren't around, I swear you'd have no life at all. You think she feels sorry for you? You think that's all there is to it?'

He pushed him roughly, half in jest, half in genuine frustration, and the younger boy, who was also the smaller of the two, almost rolled off the unbarred edge of their domain. He let out a yelp of fear and scrabbled quickly back to safety.

'Ajit! Yao! Stop that right now!'

Both flinched with guilt and looked around. The house was only twenty metres away, and they could see their mother looking out of the kitchen window, frowning threateningly at them.

'Your father already warned you—no skylarking in the tree-house or down it comes for good. Do you *want* to fall to your death?'

The boys looked at the grass a scant two metres below, rolled their eyes at each other, and said together, 'No, Maa.'

It did not satisfy her, or perhaps even at that distance she caught the eye-roll.

'Kwame!' she called. 'The boys are idle.'

'Are they?' her husband answered. 'How fortunate for me. I could use the help of two sturdy youngsters. Come!'

Each shooting the other 'this is *your* fault' glares, they climbed down from the tree and walked up the hill to where their father was digging a drainage trench for the garden.

He grinned at them. 'The pick and spade are too big for your hands, but you can move those stones out of the way for me. Stack them over there . . . and down there. We can mend the terrace with them later on.'

The grin did not fool them; their father had a pleasant yet implacable manner, and the more pleasant he was, the less likely it would be that he could be persuaded from his path. They set to work, Yao flinching slightly in the bright sunlight now that he was out from under the shade of the tree. His father took off his own hat and dropped it, oversized and sweaty, onto the boy's head. Then he squatted comfortably nearby and occasionally pointed out where he wanted the stones placed.

'What were you quarrelling about?' he asked.

'We weren't quarrelling,' said the elder in disgust.

'Ajit was talking about who's Maa's favourite,' said the younger, looking with narrowed eyes at his brother from under the hat's shady brim.

'Not about who's *my* favourite?' their father said, pretending to be disappointed.

'Oh, I know Ajit's yours,' Yao replied offhandedly.

The words had an odd effect. Speaking with a dangerous courtesy, his father said, 'May I know why?'

'Because he looks just like you,' said Yao innocently while Ajit covered his face with a dust-whitened hand and groaned.

'Boys, leave the stones a moment,' said his father in a surprising gentle voice, so gentle in fact that Yao finally realised that he might have said something wrong.

Kwame pulled the boys to sit down on either side of him and said, 'You don't look at your own face, Yao. You're the one who looks like me, not Ajit.'

He paused and fondly traced the line of his son's brow and jaw with his fingers. 'My facial structure, my nose. Even the shape of the eyes is mine, though that purple colour isn't anyone's fault.'

He tweaked Yao's nose, and the boy's habitually serious face broke into a rare smile.

'Now Ajit doesn't really look like your Maa, but if you could only remember what your Grandda looked like, you'd realise he's the image of Semwe. Except for those hairy arms—we can't account for them,' and he dropped a light, playful punch on Ajit's shoulder as the lad grinned up at him, his deep black eyes twinkling.

'But I don't like this talk of favourites, and I'll tell you why. There was a man . . . his name was Ansige.'

He paused for a moment and looked very thoughtful, almost sad.

'I never met Ansige, but he was the sort of person you get to hear quite a lot about. He was the son of a chief's daughter, but his father did not acknowledge him. People say he used to pass Ansige on the street as if he didn't know him. Ansige used to eat as much as twenty men until at last he ate himself to death. At first I thought he was a weak man, a sick man, but later, after I learned about his past, I wondered if perhaps he was just hungry for recognition. I promised myself I would never do that to my own sons.'

There was a slightly baffled silence. The twins gave each other the wide-eyed look that youngsters get when a parental lecture becomes a bit too complicated. Kwame caught it, smiled ruefully, and gave them the brief man-hug that a father uses on his sons.

'You are both mine,' he summarised. 'I may understand Ajit's sense of humour a little better than I can grasp Yao's deep thoughts, but you're still both mine.'

'And mine, too,' came a voice behind them.

There was Paama, smiling approvingly at her husband, a tray of tall glasses in her hands. Their sides were cloudy with condensation, but the pale greenish-brown liquid inside them was too familiar to be mistaken.

'Ginger and lime!' said Ajit, jumping up for his share.

'Good of you to be so quick, dear. Now take this glass to your father and then come back for yours,' she said smoothly.

Kwame accepted his drink with a broad smile at the family joke. 'I was just telling the boys a true story about a less fortunate son . . . and speaking of true stories, why don't you tell them about the exciting life you led just before you met me?'

Paama's gaze flickered quickly over her sons as they took their drinks, and she said, 'I don't think we need to bother with that old story any more.'

Ajit eyed his brother over the rim of his glass and waggled his eyebrows meaningfully. *She knows.*

'Why not?' Yao said, glaring at his brother. 'We'd love to hear it.'

Paama gave him a look that was at once so knowing and so amused that he gulped lime and ginger juice the wrong way. He choked and wheezed helplessly as his father and his brother laughed at the turning colours of his face.

'Take him inside and flush out his lungs,' Kwame advised, taking pity on him at last.

Paama took the empty glasses back on the tray and walked Yao back to the house. Once inside, she made him drink a glass of goat's milk to soothe the irritation of the ginger, and then she passed him a honey-almond cake for the sake of comfort. He stood beside her at the window while she washed the dishes, and gazed outside, watching Ajit as he helped his father continue work on the trench.

Suddenly he felt very jealous.

'I wish I could stay out in the sun,' he said angrily.

'But you can't,' she replied with calm. 'Not with your skin the colour it is.'

Yao did not ask why. He had asked why many years ago when he first struggled under the discipline of covering clothes, sheltering hats, and carefully timed outdoor sessions. Instead he said, 'If I could choose, I'd want my skin to be . . . blue. A really deep, dark blue.'

'Indigo,' his mother clarified. 'Yes, I bet you would.'

He did not look up at her, but he leaned against her in that affectionate way sons have with their mothers when they feel they are too old for all that babyish hugging and kissing. She leaned against him too, and splashed him with the dishwater, whether accidentally or on purpose he couldn't tell, but the smile she flashed him was mischievous.

'Your father and I have been thinking about travelling again. The Sisters have taught you all that a lay person can know, and it's time you boys were apprenticed anyway. What do you think?'

'I'd love to see what else there is besides Makendha,' Yao said with enthusiasm. 'As for being an apprentice...I know Ajit wants to be a tracker like Da,' he added a little wistfully.

She glanced at him. Her face was sympathetic, but not pitying. 'I'll teach you how to cook if you like. No need to be out in the sun for that.'

'Yes!' he exclaimed, thrilled at the idea. Though he was her son and had grown up eating at her table daily, he was not immune to Paama's fame as a cook. 'When can we start?'

'Today if you like. What would you like to make?'

He did not have to think for very long. The memory came to him, as the memories often did, although he found it impossible to discuss them with anyone except his twin brother.

'Chocolate cake,' he declared.

Paama guided him through the recipe that very evening. It went rather well. He even tried a slice of the end result on Constancy, the family cat, and she too seemed to agree that he might yet have a future in the art of providing humans with sustenance.

Karen Lord was born in Barbados in 1968 and decided to explore the world. After completing a science degree at the University of Toronto, she realised that the course she had enjoyed most was History of the English Language. Several degrees, jobs, countries, and years later, she had taught physics, trained soldiers, worked in the Foreign Service, and gained a PhD in sociology of religion. She writes fiction to balance the nonfiction she produces as an academic and research consultant. She lives in Barbados and now uses the internet to explore the world, which is cheaper.

ACKNOWLEDGEMENTS

To Dr Peter Laurie, for reading the very first draft, giving me excellent advice, and recommending that I enter the manuscript in the Frank Collymore Literary Competition; to the Reverend Dr Carol Roberts, for proofreading my PhD thesis and *Redemption in Indigo* and doing a brilliant job with both; to the Frank Collymore Literary Endowment Committee, whose award supported me both emotionally and financially as I strove to take my writing more seriously; to Nalo Hopkinson, for bringing the news of a local award to an international audience, and for continuing to promote Caribbean speculative fiction, not least through the example of her own award-winning works; to Small Beer Press, for accepting this manuscript; to Robert Edison Sandiford and other authors, for directly or indirectly helping me to navigate the business side of a writing career; to my father and my sister, for more than I can express; and to everyone—friends, family and strangers—for reading drafts, giving feedback, and keeping my muse motivated with their enthusiasm and interest, to all of you I say, 'Thank you'.

Since 2001, Small Beer Press, an independent publishing house, has published satisfying and surreal novels and short story collections by award-winning writers and exciting talents whose names you may never have heard, but whose work you'll never be able to forget. Recent titles include:

JULIA HOLMES, *Meeks: A Novel*
"A wild, woolly, sly, gentle and wry first novel. . . . It's a book whose singular vision keeps returning to me at odd moments, one of the most original and readable novels that's come my way in a long time."—*The New York Times Book Review* | Editor's Choice

KAREN JOY FOWLER, *What I Didn't See and Other Stories*
"A volume that serves as a fine introduction to Fowler, if you haven't come across her before—and one that will deeply satisfy fans who've been with her from the beginning."
—*Seattle Times*

KATHE KOJA, *Under the Poppy: A Novel*
A Victorian brothel. A love triangle. A vivid, sexy, historical novel that zips along like the best guilty pleasure. "Love and betrayal, blackmail and beatings, sex and death . . . Koja's language is at its poetic best."—Cory Doctorow (*BoingBoing*)

TED CHIANG, *Stories of Your Life and Others*
"Shining, haunting, mind-blowing tales . . . this collection is a pure marvel. Chiang is so exhilarating so original so stylish he just leaves you speechless."
—Junot Díaz (author of *The Brief Wondrous Life of Oscar Wao*)

JOAN AIKEN, *The Serial Garden: The Complete Armitage Family Stories* (BIG MOUTH HOUSE)
HOLLY BLACK, *The Poison Eaters and Other Stories* (BIG MOUTH HOUSE)
POPPY Z. BRITE, *Second Line: Two Short Novels of Love and Cooking in New Orleans*
GEORGES-OLIVIER CHATEAUREYNAUD, *A Life on Paper* (trans. EDWARD GAUVIN)
KELLY ESKRIDGE, *Solitaire*
GREER GILMAN, *Cloud & Ashes: Three Winter's Tales* (Tiptree Award Winner)
ALASDAIR GRAY, *Old Men in Love: John Tunnock's Posthumous Papers*
KELLY LINK, *Magic for Beginners*; *Stranger Things Happen*; *Trampoline* (Editor)
VINCENT MCCAFFREY, *Hound: A Novel*
BENJAMIN PARZYBOK, *Couch: A Novel*
GEOFF RYMAN, *The King's Last Song: a novel*; *Paradise Tales*; *The Child Garden*
DELIA SHERMAN & CHRISTOPHER BARZAK (Eds.), *Interfictions 2*
A Working Writer's Daily Planner 2011: Your Year in Writing

LADY CHURCHILL'S ROSEBUD WRISTLET
A twice-yearly fiction &c. zine ("Tiny, but celebrated"—*Washington Post*) edited by Kelly Link & Gavin J. Grant publishing writers such as Carol Emshwiller, Karen Joy Fowler, David J. Schwartz, Molly Gloss, and many others. (*The Best of LCRW* is available from Del Rey.) A multitude of subscription options—including chocolate—are available on our website.

Read excerpts, follow our trail, find out more at

WWW.SMALLBEERPRESS.COM